Adventures of the Longevity Mystery Club

Arlene R. Taylor, PhD & Sharlet M. Briggs, PhD
Illustrations by Seth Foley

Publishers Reminder

This book is not a medical, psychological, or biological text. The information and resources herein are for general educational and informational purposes only and do not present an in-depth treatment of specific research findings or topics. They are not intended to take the place of professional counseling, medical or psychological care, recovery therapy, or personalized recommendations from healthcare professionals.

The publisher, author, contributors, certified facilitators, volunteers, and editors expressly disclaim all responsibility and any liability (direct or indirect) for adverse effects, (actual or perceived), from the use or misuse of concepts presented herein.

If you find errors or typos in this book, please know that they serve a purpose—a few brains really enjoy searching for mistakes.

Adventures of the Longevity Mystery Club

Arlene R. Taylor, PhD & Sharlet M. Briggs, PhD
Illustrations by Seth Foley
Success Resources International, Napa, CA, USA

Adventures of the Longevity Mystery Club

Requests for information should be addressed to:

www.ArleneTaylor.org
www.thrivingbrain.com
www.LongevityLivestyleMatters.com

ISBN 1-887307-17-6

Special thanks to Michelle Nash, Brenda L. Balding, and Connor Gerber

Illustrations: Seth Foley www.sfoleystudios.com

Cover design and book production: David O. Eastman

Printed in the United States

Table of Contents

Dedication

Adventures of the Longevity Mystery Club is dedicated to Connor, who reads all the *Adventures* manuscripts and offers suggestions—and to children everywhere whose lives can improve through an enhanced understanding of the brain in general and theirs in particular. And it can be so much fun!

Prologue

Summer vacation has finally arrived and the granddaughters of Dr. Briggs, Aimi and Stella, along with their friends Tad and Toni (who are twins) and their cousin Connor are foot-loose and fancy-free. The children are clamoring to have an adventure. So along with their new club sponsor, Grami, they set out to do just that. Their number one dog, Buddy-the-Beagle, tags along whenever possible! Another book in the Adventures Series, *Adventures of the Longevity Mystery Club* or the *LM Club*, provides brain-function and health-education information through stories about the children's many summer adventures and how they can stay healthier and younger for longer—and have fun in the process.

Toni, Grami, Tad, & Connor

Aimi, Stella, & Grami

Five little friends wanted lots of summer fun,
And starting a Club they were sure was #1.
When Grami agreed their club sponsor to be,
They were set for adventures of, well, you'll see.

Foreword

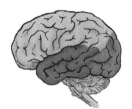 Brain-function information wasn't readily available half a century ago. Not even a quarter of a century ago—at least not at today's level in this, the "Age of the Brain."

Knowing more about the brain in general (and *your* brain in particular) has amazing potential—not only to keep your brain and what carries it around (your body) as healthy and functional as possible but also to increase your likelihood of success. When practically applied, knowledge is power.

When the brain-based program *Longevity Lifestyle Matters* was created, readers and program attendees alike inquired about whether similar information was available for children. A typical remark was, "If I'd been exposed to this information during my childhood, I'm quite sure some of my choices would have been different."

By way of response, the challenge of translating brain-function information into easily understood, bite-sized chunks accessible to the average child's brain gave birth to this book: *Adventures of the Longevity Mystery Club.* The information is conveyed through stories since studies have shown that human brains all over the world typically love stories and tend to learn through them quickly.

A study of pregnant women who read aloud a specific paragraph of a children's story three times a day for the last six weeks of their pregnancy shows that the infants, after their birth, preferred to listen to the passage their mothers had read during the third trimester. They had become familiar with certain sounds while in utero and associated those tones with comfort and security.

Following are a few research-study conclusions:

- Reading aloud to the baby will do far more to develop a love of reading than packs of flash cards. This is especially true if reading is associated with a loving environment and parental (adult) enjoyment. (Jane M. Healy, PhD, *Your Child's Growing Mind*)

- Cognitive stimulation, i.e. reading books or going to a museum, reduces the likelihood for attention challenges later in life. (Wendy Sue Swanson, MD, MBE, "What Does TV Do to My Kid's Brain?")

- Teenagers who spend more time reading books (as compared to listening to contemporary music) seem to experience less depression. (*Archives of Pediatric and Adolescent Medicine*)

- The single most important activity for building knowledge required for eventual success in reading is reading aloud to children at home and in the classroom. It is deemed more important than worksheets, homework, assignments, book reports, and flashcards. (Jim Trelease, *The Read-Aloud Handbook*, 7th edition)

- Reading aloud to children ultimately improves *their* reading, in addition to their writing, speaking, and listening skills and, best of all, their attitudes about reading. (Geneen Roth, *When Food Is Love*)

To this end, *The Longevity Mystery Club* presents brain-function information in story format featuring Aimi, Stella, Connor, Toni and Tad, and Grami. This book can be used as an adjunct to the *Longevity Lifestyle Matters* program or free-standing in almost any setting. As an adult, if you are reading or listening to the book *Longevity Lifestyle Matters* yourself, try comparing notes with your children or grandchildren about their book version and chat about what each of you is learning about staying younger and healthier for longer. What they learn now, in childhood, *matters*—and your participation impacts those positive outcomes.

This book is available in paperback, eBook, CD audiobook, and MP3 options.

Happy reading!

—The Authors

The littlest of the sleuthing five,
And ever so happy to be alive,
Miss Stella saw her 'bent' unfurl—
When she became a gumshoe girl.

1—Mascot Sleuth

"Grami!" said Aimi in her soft, sweet voice. "It's summer vacation, you know. Stella and I want to go on an adventure. So do the twins, Tad and Toni, and so does their cousin Connor. Can we all go on an adventure?"

Before Grami could reply, Stella interrupted. "What is a sen-ten-tun-air-ee-an? I want to *know*."

"Do you mean a *centenarian*?" asked Grami.

"I guess," Stella said, uncertainly.

"A centenarian is a person who is at least 100 years old," said Aimi. "Our teacher said there are lots of people around the world who are centenarians."

"There are." said Grami. "And there are also supercentenarians, typically defined as individuals who live to be 110 years old or older. Reportedly one lady was 119 years old when she died in something like 1999."

"Wow!" cried Stella. "A very very *very* old lady! Did you meet her, Grami? I want to *know*."

"I heard that, Stella," said Connor, coming in from the back yard where he and Tad had been playing with the rabbits. "How old do you think Grami is, anyway?"

"Well, Grami *was* alive in 1999," said Toni.

Connor laughed. "Good point, Toni. I was thinking about supercentenarians—not about the year 1999."

"I wonder where these centenarians and supercentenarians live," mused Tad.

1

"Yes, where?" asked Stella. "I want to *know*."

"Perhaps you'd enjoy doing detective work about centenarians and supercentenarians," suggested Grami.

"I'd like to do some detective work," said Connor.

"So would I," said Aimi, in her soft voice.

"Count me in," said Toni.

"And me!" cried Stella, in her not-so-soft voice. "I may be the littlest, but count me in, too!" She was so excited she clapped her hands, jumped up in the air, and twirled three times.

"We can all be detectives," said Tad. "I'd like to be a detective."

"If you want to be detectives," said Grami, "your first 'detecting' job could be researching information about centenarians and even about superercentenarians."

"Well, if we're going to be detectives, we should start a club," said Connor.

"What a good idea!" exclaimed Toni. "Then we'll need a club name."

"Let's call it the *Centenarian Club*," suggested Stella. "For people who are very very *very* old."

"But we're not centenarians," said Tad. "We're just researching information about people who are centenarians or supercentenarians. How about *The Five Gumshoes*."

"I don't want *gum* on *my* shoes!" cried Stella.

"Stella," said Tad, patiently. "The word *gumshoes* is just another name for a detective."

"Oh, good," sighed Stella. "I definitely do not want gum on my shoes!"

"You could call it *Club Detective*," said Grami.

"What are words for being very old or living a long time?" asked Toni.

"Ancient, senior, aged, venerable," said Grami. "Also, long-lived and maybe . . . longevity."

"That's it!" cried Toni. "What about the *Longevity Club*? We can research how to live a long time."

"But detectives solve mysteries," said Connor. "There's nothing in that name about mysteries."

"We could call it the *Longevity Mystery Club,*" said Aimi. "It's a mystery how to live a long time."

"In one way it *is* a mystery," said Grami. "In another, research is uncovering some of the mysteries."

"I like that name," said Connor. "The *LM Club*, for short."

"Good idea," said Tad.

"It's got a good ring to it," said Toni.

Stella nodded. "And we need a club song, too!"

"You like to make up songs, Aimi," said Tad. "Would you compose a club song for our new *LM Club*?"

"Do you think I could do that?" asked Aimi.

"Absolutely, you can," said Grami.

"Okay," said Aimi. "I'll start composing a club song. Or maybe two." She laughed.

"I'm quite sure your ukulele teacher would be willing to help you write out the music," said Grami, "and even give you some tips."

Just then the sound of a howling commotion came from Grami's back yard. A real racket.

"Uh-oh," said Stella. "That's Buddy-the-Beagle's *I-want-to-be-with-you* howl."

When Stella opened the back door, Buddy-the-Beagle catapulted into the room, as if he'd just been shot from a cannon. His little tail wagged furiously back and forth, back and forth. He looked at Grami and at each of the five detectives. Then he sat down in the middle of the room, threw back his head, stuck his little nose in the air, and howled and howled and howled.

"That's Buddy-the-Beagle's *I'm-so happy* howl," said Connor, who had been listening carefully.

"I think he wants to join our *LM Club*!" cried Stella, speaking even more loudly than usual to be heard over the howling din.

"He cannot be a member of our *LM Club*," said Tad seriously, shaking his head. "Buddy-the-Beagle is a *dog*."

"Not so fast, Tad," said Connor. "Remember what Lenny told us. You know, the short old man at the Bay & Howl Animal Shelter. The one with a very big nose and only three hairs on his head."

"I remember Lenny," Tad began, "but . . ." His voice trailed off.

"Lenny told us many things," Aimi said, sweetly. "There were way too many things to remember, that's what. I know. I was there."

"Remind us, Connor," said Grami, smiling.

"Lenny said that beagles are number two after bloodhounds in their ability to smell. The scent area in a beagle's brain is 40 times larger than the scent area in a human's brain. That means Buddy-the-Beagle's sense of smell is thousands of times stronger than ours. My brain's  opinion is that having a superb sense of smell makes him a detective."

"You copied Grami's expression," said Toni, laughing. "Grami says, 'My brain's opinion.'"

Aimi and Stella, Tad and Toni, and Connor looked at Grami. "What do you think, Grami?" asked Stella. "Can Buddy-the-Beagle be a member of our new *LM Club*? I want to *know*."

Grami thought for a long minute. Finally she said, "I agree with Tad. The *Longevity Mystery Club* is for you five children—human detectives—and Buddy-the-Beagle is definitely a dog, so he cannot be a member. However," she continued, holding up her hand for them to wait, "I also agree with Connor. And I have an idea."

"What is it?" cried Stella. "I want to *know*!"

"I think Buddy-the-Beagle could be the club mascot," said Grami. "Many clubs have a mascot."

"What is a mass-kot?" asked Stella. "Is it a lot of little beds? I want to *know*."

"It's a symbol selected to represent an organization or club," said Grami. "The mascot for the United States Navy, for example, is a goat. The Olympics and Para-Olympics have mascots. Many organizations do."

"A mascot is a great idea," said Toni.

"I agree," said Tad.

"I think a dog with a superb sense of smell would make a good mascot for our *LM Club*," said Connor, grinning from ear to ear.

"Oh, do let's have Buddy-the-Beagle be our mascot!" cried Stella. She was so excited she clapped her hands, jumped up in the air, and twirled three times. The roly-poly little puppy watched Stella. Then he threw back his head, stuck up his little nose, opened his little mouth, and howled his *I'm-so-happy* howl.

"And a sponsor," said Connor. "A club needs a sponsor, too. I think Grami would make the *best* sponsor."

"Will you be our sponsor?" asked Stella. "I want to *know*!"

Grami smiled and nodded. "I'd love to be club sponsor and plan some adventures." The five *LM Club* members clapped with pleasure.

"What are we doing to do first?" asked Aimi.

"Let me think for a minute," said Grami. All five children were very still. Even little Buddy-the-Beagle closed his mouth and made not one sound. "I have it," said Grami, presently. "I have an idea. As your *LM Club* sponsor, I hereby declare that your first detective adventure will happen tomorrow morning."

"Tomorrow morning?" cried Stella. "What is the detective adventure? I want to *know*."

"The adventure is a secret," said Grami. "Just be here at ten o'clock sharp."

"Can we start at nine o'clock?" asked Aimi.

Grami shook her head. "You are all taking music lessons this summer. Emotional Intelligence—your EQ—suggests that it's better to get your practicing done first thing in the morning. That way we don't have to hurry back from any of our adventures so you can practice. Besides, you may be tired and hungry by the time we get home."

"I'll practice my recorder," said Connor.

"Me too," said Toni. "I have new songs to learn."

"I'll practice my ukulele, I will," said Stella.

"I'd much rather practice my guitar in the morning," said Tad. "I'll be hungry when we get home and will want to eat. Not practice my guitar."

"I will start on a club song," said Aimi, smiling

"That about covers it," said Grami.

Promptly at ten o'clock the next morning, five LM Club members got into Grami's car and clicked their seatbelts. Grami started the car and they were on their way.

"Here we are," said Grami a few minutes later as she parked the car near a large gray building.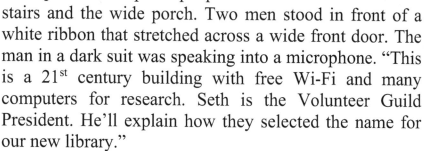

"Look at those humongous lions," said Aimi, pointing at two crouching cement lions that guarded the steps leading up to the wide porch. Groups of people were on the stairs and the wide porch. Two men stood in front of a white ribbon that stretched across a wide front door. The man in a dark suit was speaking into a microphone. "This is a 21st century building with free Wi-Fi and many computers for research. Seth is the Volunteer Guild President. He'll explain how they selected the name for our new library."

Before Stella could ask any questions, Grami whispered, "A *guild* is an organization of people who have similar interests. In this case, the new library."

Seth, Volunteer Guild President, took the microphone, cleared his throat, and began to speak. "First, '*Neo*' means new. Remember that. This 21st century building is new."

"That is very obvious," Connor whispered to Tad.

"Second, '*Leo*' is the Latin word for lion. Remember that, too. A local artist donated our magnificent  crouching cement lions, which got us thinking about parks: wild animal parks, skate-board parks, dog parks, and national parks. Third, we began to realize that this library project is a type of park, too. This new 21st century building is filled with words: written, printed, and heard; in books, on computers, and DVDs. Words you can see with your eyes, hear with your ears, and feel with your fingers. You can learn with words, play games with words, and communicate with words, using sign language or speaking in your regular voice."

"That's a lot of words," said Stella, aloud.

Aimi poked her and whispered, "Hush, Stella." *"Puleese.* Just listen." Stella nodded and listened.

"When the Volunteer Guild was asked to select a name," Seth continued, "we knew what we wanted." He paused a moment for dramatic effect. "The Volunteer Guild chose a unique 21st century name. The decision was unanimous."

Seth handed the microphone back to the man in the dark suit. A murmur of excitement ran through the people assembled on the stairs and the wide front porch.

"What name did they choose?" asked Stella, impatiently. "I want to *know*."

This time it was Grami who whispered, "Just listen, Stella. You'll find out."

"Thank you, Seth," said the man in the dark suit. Taking scissors from his jacket pocket, he cut the white ribbon. Seth pulled on a small rope that raised a curtain, uncovering big brass letters above the wide front door. "I hereby declare the Neo-Leo Wordpark officially open," said the man in the dark suit. He punched several numbers into a key pad beside the wide front door, and it swung wide open. "Come on in," he said. "We hope you visit often." Every one clapped and clapped.

"I like the name," said Aimi, as they followed the people into the new 21st Century building. "I really like the name Neo-Leo Wordpark. It's fun, easy to remember, and a new 21st century title."

"I like it, too," said Grami. "It is very unique." Once inside, the five detectives and their sponsor looked around. "He wasn't kidding," whispered Grami. "Just look at all those computers."

"You can stop whispering, Grami," Connor said. "Seth said you can talk in a regular voice."

"That will take some getting used to," said Grami. "When I was young, we always had to whisper in a library. "I dropped a book on the floor once by accident, and the librarian actually asked me to *leave* the building!"

Grami chuckled, remembering. "Now I can speak in a regular voice at the Neo-Leo Wordpark. I like it."

"What is a Li-bri-vox Zone?" asked Stella, reading a sign that sat on top of the counter. "I want to *know*."

"Librivox is the name of an organization that creates audiobooks," explained one of the guild volunteers who had overheard Stella's question. "Librivox volunteers read books that are in the public domain. That is, books that are owned by everyone because they were written a long time ago. This entire Neo-Leo Wordpark is a Librivox Zone, meaning you can read out loud and listen to audiobooks in private cubicles, and talk anywhere in a regular voice. We'd appreciate it, however, if you avoid whistling or singing or shouting."

"Thank you," said Stella, politely. "I've already learned two new words today: *Wordpark* and *Librivox*!"

"We have two hours to spend at the Neo-Leo Wordpark," said Grami. "I suggest you select a computer and start using the Internet. When we get back to my place, you can have your first official meeting of the Longevity Mystery Club and share what you've learned."

"I want to research something new and *fun* about su-per-cen-ten-ar-ians," said Stella. "Sit here with me, Grami. We can research together."

"Having fun while researching is key to being a good detective. I brought something to help you," Grami said. Reaching into her bag, she took out five pens and five notebooks. "When you discover something interesting, jot it down in your *My Sleuth Notebook*."

"What's a sl-oo-th?" asked Stella. "I want to *know*."

"It's another name for a detective," said Grami.

"I want to sleuth out where that centenarian lady lived in France," said Aimi.

"I'm sleuthing Leo,'" said Tad.

"I want to sleuth something about beagles," said Connor. "Something I don't already know."

"I'm sleuthing longevity," said Toni. "After all, it's part of our club name."

It seemed only a short time before the five detectives heard Grami say, "Detectives, it's time to go."

"Those two hours went by really fast," said Aimi. "Guess that's what happens when you're having fun."

They got back into the car for the ride home.

Back at the house, five detectives, their sponsor, and their mascot—energetically howling his *I'm-so-happy* song—gathered in Grami's study. Settling into her favorite chair, Grami asked, "What did you discover today at the Neo-Leo Wordpark?"

"How many names are there for a detective?" asked Stella, interrupting. "Besides *Sl-oo-th* and *Gum-on-your-shoe*, that is. I want to *know*."

"Several," said Grami, chuckling. "*Private Eye* and *Shadow,* to name two."

"Write down those four synonyms in your *My Sleuth Notebook*," suggested Toni.

"Okay," said Stella. "And I'll find more next time we go to the Neo-Leo Wordpark."

"I learned something new about beagles," said Connor, curled up in his favorite beanbag.

Opening his *My Sleuth Notebook*, he read aloud: "Beagles are merry and fun loving. But because they are hounds they need patient, creative training. Their noses guide them through life. They are never happier than when following an interesting scent."

"That describes our Buddy-the-Beagle," said Grami. "He loves to sniff and sniff and sniff some more."

"He's our sniffing sleuth mascot," said Stella.

Connor continued. "Beagles enjoy playing tracking games. Ask your dog to sit-stay outside while you walk through the grass to leave a scent trail. Put a small treat at the end of the trail. Then retrace your steps and release your beagle to find the treat. That lets them play and have fun while doing something they are good at doing."

"Good idea," said Grami.

"Let's do that," said Stella.

"We need to use small healthy treats," said Connor. "Remember, fat dogs are not healthy dogs."

"Seth was right" said Tad. "*Leo* is the Latin word for lion. It's also the name for something else. Leo is the name for a constellation that looks like a crouching lion, like the crouching cement lions at the Neo-Leo Wordpark."

"What is a kon-STELLA-ay-shun?" interrupted Stella. "My name is in it. I want to *know*."

"It's a group of stars," said Tad, laughing. "A cluster of stars up in the sky.

"Where else would they be?" asked Toni, smiling.

"I wrote a verse about our mascot," said Tad, ignoring Toni's question. He read:

"Buddy-the-Beagle's a flatfoot dog,
Who proudly wears a mascot tog.
His sense of smell is number two,
So sniffing sleuthing he can do."

Everyone clapped; then it was Stella's turn. She opened her *My Sleuth Notebook*. "Grami and I looked up supercentenarians. We learned that a lady by the name of Sarah DeRemer Clark Knauss was born September 24, 1880 and died December 30, 1999. That's 119 years 97 days. She was an American supercentenarian and the oldest person ever from the United States."

"We also learned," added Grami, "that Sarah is the second-oldest fully documented person ever, behind the contested case of a French lady named Jeanne Louise Calment who lived in Arles, in Southern France, thought to be 122 years 164 days when she died."

"What does con-tes-ted means?" asked Stella. "I want to *know!*"

"It means that questions have recently been raised about the accuracy of documentation. Research may confirm she was actually 122 years 164 days when she died or it may be that Sarah claims that distinction at 119 years 97 days."

"Obviously, they did something right to live that long!" exclaimed Connor.

"I still remember the French words you taught me for RSVP, Grami," said Aimi. "*Répondez s'il vous plait.*"

"Those were the words on the invitation to our birthday party," said Toni. "They mean 'Please respond.'"

"You mean the anniversary of your and Tad's birthday," said Aimi. "You only have one birthday." Tad and Toni looked at each other and laughed.

"I looked up *longevity*," said Toni. "Many things can shorten a person's life: lack of sleep, dehydration, negativity, too much sitting, not enough physical exercise, head injuries, and lots of stress."

"Wow! That's a long list," said Aimi.

"Oh, that's just some of them," said Toni. "There are more: poor quality nutrition, lack of mental exercise, whining, complaining, ungratefulness, being overweight, and obesity."

"What is o-bee-city?" asked Stella. "Is it a special city just for bees? I want to *know*!"

"*Obesity* is when a person weighs too much for their height," said Toni, trying to keep her face straight.

"Grami, do you weigh too much for your height?" asked Stella. I want to *know*!"

"You're wanting to know an awful lot of things today," said Aimi, before Grami could say anything.

"Well, Stella," said Grami, "there have been times lately when I've wondered if miniature dressmaking creatures hide in my closet and sew my clothes a little tighter every night. You know, the women in my family all seem to gain weight as they age, and I just took it for granted that I'd do the same thing. But maybe not."

"I want you to be a supercentenarian!" said Stella.

Grami smiled. "Me too. I think I'll aim for that."

"Hey, Sis," said Tad, "I want to learn about things that *lengthen* my life, not shorten it, so I can study rabbits for a long time."

"That's easy," said Connor. "Just do the opposite of whatever is on Toni's list." He laughed.

"Can Emotional Intelligence help me live longer?" asked Stella. "I want to *know*."

"High levels of EQ can help you make good choices about how you live your life," said Grami, "and those decisions could help you live longer."

"Then let's research living longer and report what we learn at our next club meeting," said Aimi.

"And then we can *do* those things," said Toni. "So we can all live longer." At those words, Stella clapped her hands, jumped in the air, and twirled three times.

"Good idea," said Tad, "but right now I need to research when we can eat. I'm v-e-r-y hungry."

"From now on, your sponsor will provide lunch for everyone at our weekly *LM Club* meetings," said Grami.

"What about lunch *today*?" asked Tad. "I'm hungry *now*. Do I really have to wait to eat lunch until next week's Club meeting?"

"Lunch is already prepared," said Grami, when she had stopped laughing. "Your club sponsor planned ahead. Let's go into the kitchen and eat."

"Afterwards let's write a verse about our new *Longevity Mystery Club*," said Aimi, high-fiving the other four club members. "Tad can help us write it."

And that's exactly what they did.

15

The Longevity Mystery Club are we,
Five plus a sponsor and mascot wee.
Sleuthing is fun and we all agree—
To live as healthy as we can be.

2—Librivox Zone

"I see that the members of the *Longevity Mystery Club* are ready to leave for the Neo-Leo-Wordpark," said Grami, smiling at the five young detectives. "And you each have your *My Sleuth Notebook* and pen."

"And we're done practicing," said Aimi. "Plus, I have some ideas for a club song."

"Buddy-the-Beagle is ready to go, too," said Stella. The roly-poly little puppy thumped his tail on the floor, his pink tongue lolling from the corner of his mouth.

"Dogs cannot go to the Neo-Leo-Wordpark," said Toni. "It is not a dog park. It is for people."

"I saw a dog at the Neo-Leo-Wordpark," cried Stella. "So I promised Buddy-the-Beagle he could go."

"Yes, a seeing-eye dog was there," said Grami, "but Buddy-the-Beagle is the *LM Club* mascot, not a seeing-eye dog. I doubt an admiral of the Navy would show up at the Neo-Leo-Wordpark trailed by the Navy's mascot—a goat." Four members of the *LM Club* laughed out loud.

Stella did not laugh. "But I *promised* Buddy-the-Beagle he could come," she said. "And you said to always do what you promise."

"I did," said Grami. "I also said to be very careful to promise only what you are sure you can deliver." She smiled at Stella. Stella did not smile back at Grami. "Did you call the Neo-Leo-Wordpark and ask if Buddy-the-Beagle could go with you?" asked Grami. "Without prior permission, he must stay home."

The littlest detective shook her head. "No, I did not call the Neo-Leo-Wordpark to ask if Buddy-the-Beagle could go with us." Stella looked at Buddy-the-Beagle. "I'm so sorry that you'll have to stay home," she said, bursting into tears. At that, the roly-poly little puppy threw back his head, pointed his little nose in the air, opened his little mouth, and began to howl.

"Did Buddy-the-Beagle understand what Stella said?" asked Toni. "That's his *I'm-sorry-for-myself* howl."

"I doubt he understood the words," said Grami, "but I'll bet he picked up on the tone of Stella's voice."

"Plus Buddy-the-Beagle doesn't like it when Stella cries," said Aimi. "I think it makes him feel bad."

"Hey, that's enough," said Tad, covering his ears. "Put a plug in it. Your howling is too much."

Buddy-the-Beagle did not put a plug in it. He just keep on howling and howling and howling.

Finally Grami said, "Tad is right. This howling is too much. Stella, please put that roly-poly little puppy out on the screened-in back porch and give him a doggie treat to keep him busy while we go to the Neo-Leo-Wordpark.

Stella picked up Buddy-the-Beagle. She put her right hand under his little bottom and used her left hand to support his chest just like Lenny had taught them at the Bay & Howl Animal Shelter. The puppy's little front legs hung down on either side of her hand. The minute she picked him up, the howling stopped.

"Uh-oh," said Aimi. "Buddy-the-Beagle thinks he's coming with us because Stella picked him up."

A few minutes later, Stella was back. "Buddy-the-Beagle is busy with his treat, so let's go."

Grami and the five detectives got into the car. "What are you planning to research today?" she asked, backing the car out of the driveway and pointing it in the direction of the Neo-Leo-Wordpark.

"We have decided to begin by researching factors related to longevity," said Connor. "We'll collect data from different websites and share the results so our sleuthing is less fragmented. And then…"

"Day-ta?" asked Stella, interrupting. "What is day-ta? And frag-men-ted? What does that mean? I want to *know*."

"I can answer that now that I'm no longer covering my ears to shut out Buddy-the-Beagle's pitiful howling," said Tad. Everyone laughed—except Stella, that is. She did not laugh. "When something is fragmented," Tad continued, "it is divided into separate parts and may even be quite disorganized. Like pieces of a jig-saw puzzle when you dump them out of the box. Or like a glass jar when it falls and shatters on cement."

"Yes," said Toni. "And when you've put all the puzzle pieces together, it is no longer fragmented. But when a glass jar shatters, you can't put the pieces back together again. It's like Humpty-Dumpty."

"And all the king's horses and all the king's men couldn't put Humpty-Dumpty together again," said Stella. "I *know* that verse."

"*Data* is a term for bits of information," said Connor. "We'll begin collecting data information, starting with Toni's list of factors that could shorten a person's life span."

"I want to research how mindset impacts a person's energy," said Tad."

"Good idea," said Grami as she parked the car near the large gray 21st century building.

On the steps of the Neo-Leo-Wordpark, Stella paused by one of the large crouching cement lions. "Too bad Buddy-the-Beagle isn't a Leo," she sighed. "He could wait here quietly beside this Leo while we're inside the Neo-Leo Wordpark sleuthing—instead of staying all alone on the screened-in back porch."

"Dream on, Stella," said Connor. "If Buddy-the-Beagle were a Leo, I'm quite sure he would not sit quietly next to a large crouching cement lion."

"I know," said Stella. "It was just wishful thinking. Grami, could we eat lunch in the park when we are done sleuthing? Buddy-the-Beagle could come with us to the park and have a doggie adventure sniffing and sniffing."

"Do the *LM Club* members want to vote on that suggestion?" asked Grami.

"We vote *yes*," cried the other four detectives in unison. With that decided, five sleuths and one sponsor climbed the rest of the stairs to the wide porch and disappeared into the Neo-Leo-Wordpark. Once inside, each detective selected a computer. Once again Stella asked Grami to sit beside her at the next computer.

"I'm making a list of words for detectives. Look," said Stella, handing her *My Sleuth Notebook* to Grami.

Grami read: "A detective is a person whose job it is to find information about someone or something. That's correct, Stella, and I see you already have four synonyms: Gumshoe, Private Eye, Sleuth, and Shadow. Perhaps you can find a couple more today."

The two hours at the Neo-Leo-Wordpark went by quickly. "Time flies when we're having fun," said Aimi, when it was time to leave. "I like sleuthing at the Neo-Leo Wordpark!"

When they were back in the car and on their way to pick up Buddy-the-Beagle and pack lunch in the brown wicker basket, Stella said, "I added three more words to my list: Tail, Nark, and Investigator. Maybe I'll be an in-ves-ti-ga-tor when I grow up."

Grami smiled down at Stella. This time Stella smiled back.

"I can hardly wait to hear what you all discovered today," said Grami, as she unpacked the brown wicker basket that Tad and Connor had carried from the car to the picnic table in the park. "Who wants to start?"

"I do," said Tad. "I looked up *negativity*. Did you know that a negative mindset can drain your energy and make you tired? Negative thoughts can increase anxiety and depression, suppress your immune system, and trigger the release of stress hormones like adrenalin and cortisol. They can even lower your sense of self-esteem. On the other hand, a *positive* mindset and *positive* thoughts can do the opposite. They can increase your energy levels, help you feel good about yourself, and strengthen your immune system. A strong immune system can help you stay well."

"I like to jazzercise," said Toni. "And that takes a lot of energy. So I need to think positive thoughts all day long."

"I learned that every thought you think alters chemicals in your brain and body," said Grami. "I did not realize that a negative mindset can be as dangerous as a germ or virus. It can harm your health, disrupt personal relationships, and contribute to failure. I'm creating a *positive* mindset, I am."

"I read about a man named Jon Gordon. He wrote a book about energy," said Tad. "I wrote something he said in *My Sleuth Notebook*. Listen: 'Think positively about the day ahead and you increase your mental and physical energy. Instead of being fearful and anxious, causing a release of stress hormones, thinking positively about the day will send positive energy to your body supplying you with sustained energy.'"

"Wow," said Grami as she set out slices of watermelon and bottles of cold lemonade along with her usual peanut butter and jam, peanut butter and jelly, and egg-salad sandwiches on white bread. And at least three kinds of cookies, of course. "We all need energy, especially as we get older."

"I looked up definitions for *mindset* so we could all be on the same page," said Connor, opening his *Notebook*. "I wrote down two definitions. Here's one: 'A *mindset* is a mental attitude that predetermines your responses; a set of opinions about something that strongly influences your inclinations and your behaviors. Everything starts in the brain and it begins with a mindset.' The second definition says this: 'Your *mindset* establishes your direction. It tells you where you are going on the map of your life. It actually *is* a map inside your brain. Each day you make many small decisions that move you along your map either toward or away from your goals.'"

"A map inside your brain," said Aimi. "How fun!" She paused. "Grami, I read something I don't understand. It was something about the brain liking congruity."

"What is con-grew-i-tea?" asked Stella. "Is it something to drink? I want to *know*."

"*Congruity* is a word that means everything is in harmony or matches," said Grami.

"Oh!" cried Stella. "Like all five *LM Club* members agreeing that you should be our sponsor, Grami. The club members had con-grew-i-tea."

"Good one," said Tad. "You nailed that comparison, Stella." The littlest sleuth smiled a very big smile.

"The brain does want congruity," Grami continued. "If you think sad thoughts, your brain searches for sad memories from the past—and you can become even sadder. If you think angry thoughts, your brain dredges up angry memories. If you think happy thoughts, your brain looks for happy memories from the past. And so on."

"And then you can be happier and happier," said Stella. "I get this con-grew-i-tea stuff." They all laughed.

"Grami, when you said people talk to themselves all the time, I didn't think I did," said Toni. "But when I closed my eyes and paid attention to what was going on inside my head, I *was* talking to myself! I was saying, 'I like being a detective and learning new things. I like the Neo-Leo-Wordpark and its computers. I like that it's a Librivox Zone.'"

"That's called self-talk," said Grami. "Your thoughts create your mindset and self-talk follows your mindset. How would you put that in your own words?"

"You talk about what you think about," said Aimi.

"And then you do what you talk about," said Toni.

"You detectives learn quickly," said Grami.

"I think about food," said Tad. "Then I talk about food. And then I eat food. Hey, I've got it!"

"And that's exactly what you are doing right now," said Grami, laughing heartily, as she watched the stack of sandwiches grow smaller and smaller.

"What did you find, Stella?" asked Grami.

"I found two *quo-ta-tions*," said Stella, talking between bites of watermelon. "One was by Henry Ford. You know he invented Ford cars and trucks," she added, importantly. "Mr. Ford said, ah, wait a minute. I wrote it in *My Sleuth Notebook*. Here it is. 'If you think you can do a thing or think you can't do a thing, you're right.' I thought I could be a detective and do research—even if I'm the littlest *LM Club* member—and I was right! Now for Mar-cus An-ton-i-us. He lived a very long time ago and I did not know him personally."

"Stella, you really have a good sense of humor," said Aimi. "I'm glad you're my little sister."

"Here's the second *quo-ta-tion,*" said Stella. She read: "The happiness of your life depends upon the quality of your thoughts. That's mindset, isn't it?"

"It sure is, Stella," said Grami. "Your thoughts create your mindset."

"Oh, I like that definition," said Connor, taking a bite out of one of Grami's cookies. "I really like what

Marcus Antonius said. May I copy that quotation from your *Notebook*?"

"Of course," said Stella, smiling broadly. She was so excited that Connor wanted to copy something from her *Notebook* that she hopped up from the picnic table, clapped her hands, jumped up in the air, and twirled three times. In all her clapping and jumping and twirling, Stella almost stepped on Buddy-the-Beagle, who had plopped himself down beside the picnic table and was panting to cool off. But she didn't. Step on him, that is. She just sat down and ate more watermelon.

"In addition to creating your mindset," said Grami, "your thoughts are so powerful they can actually reshape software in your brain. If you choose to maintain a positive attitude rather than a negative one, your brain can rewire itself to facilitate that mindset."

"And that can give you more energy," said Toni. "Everything seems to be connected with something else, doesn't it? It's so interesting."

"I read about that Marcus Antonius fellow in school," said Tad. "In English his name was Marc Antony. My teacher said he liked Cleopatra."

"Who liked Cleopatra?" asked Grami, chuckling. "Your teacher or Marc Antony?"

Tad glanced at Grami, a puzzled look on his face. Then he started to laugh. "I'll say that again, Grami, more clearly this time." Tad stood up, cleared his throat and said. "My teacher said that Marcus Antonius--or Marc Antony--liked Cleopatra." That made everybody laugh. Everyone but Buddy-the-Beagle.

"Here's the bottom line," said Grami. "Your brain can only do what it thinks it can do. If your brain thinks it can or thinks it can't, it is correct."

"How does my brain know what it can do?" asked Aimi, puzzled.

"It's your job to tell it what it can do," said Grami.

"And exactly how do you do that?" asked Connor, always intrigued about *brain stuff,* as he called it.

"You tell your brain what it can do through your self-talk," replied Grami. "Remember, self-talk follows mindset. If your mindset is positive, in all likelihood your self-talk will be positive. Naturally, the opposite is also true. If your mindset is negative, your self-talk will probably be negative, as well. Have I ever told you about the White Bear Phenomenon?"

"No," said Connor. "At least I don't think so."

"What is the White Bear Fen-om-en-on?" asked Stella. "I want to *know.*"

"We all want to know," said Aimi, "and Grami is trying to tell us, Stella, but you're talking. Again! *Puleese,* just listen."

Stella stopped talking and listened.

"I know you are interested in new things, Stella," said Grami, smiling kindly. "Tell me what you see in your mind's eye when I say: '*Don't think about the white bear.*'"

"That's easy," said Connor. "A white bear."

"Grami asked *me* what *I* saw," said Stella.

"So, answer the question already," said Connor. "What do you see?"

"Okay," said Stella. "I see a white bear."

"Grami said, '*Don't* think about the white bear,'" said Toni. "But I still picture a white bear..."

"Same here," said Aimi. "When I tell myself, 'Don't think about a white bear,' that's all I think about. One white bear after another."

"Me, too," said Tad. "Actually I see several white bears in my mind's eye."

"I can't stop thinking about it!" exclaimed Stella. "Yikes. How do I stop thinking about a white bear?"

"Think about something else," said Toni.

"Grami, if you don't want us to think about the white bear, what *do* you want us to think about?" asked Connor. "*A brown bear or a black bear?*"

"Or Buddy-the-Beagle?" asked Stella.

"Or food?" asked Tad, laughing.

"Maybe rabbits," said Connor.

"That is one of the problems with negative self-talk and negative instructions," said Grami. "Whatever you say  *first* creates a picture in your mind's eye. It's called working memory. However, it doesn't tell your brain what to do, or anyone else's brain, for that matter. Your brain often misses the 'don't' and keeps seeing the first picture. Sometimes your brain does try to convert the first picture to something else—but to what?"

"Oh my!" said Aimi, in a louder voice than usual. "I told Stella, 'Don't touch the stove,' and she touched the stove. What should I have told her? What would have been better for her brain to hear? More effective, you know."

"What do you think?" asked Grami. "You are *LM Club* members. You are detectives."

"Keep your hands away from the stove," said Toni.

"Put your hands in your pockets," said Tad.

"I get it," said Aimi. "Positive self-talk means you tell yourself what you want your brain to do instead of what you do not want it to do."

"Well said, Aimi," replied Grami.

"When you give positive instructions to others," added Connor, "you're telling them what to do, as well. This could be a much less confusing way to talk to yourself  and to others." He paused, thinking, and then asked, "Would positive instructions work with animals? Tad keeps telling his rabbits, 'Don't give me any more kits,' and guess what, Grami? They just keep giving him kits and kits and more kits..."

"What kits are you talking about?" asked Stella. "First-aid kits or shoe-polish kits? I want to *know*."

Grami laughed so hard she actually had to sit down. "Stella, baby rabbits are called *kits*. And Connor, I really think both parties need to speak the same language in order to be clearly understood. Do you speak 'bunny talk'?"

"Not hardly," said Connor, also laughing. "I was joking, you know." Grami nodded, still chuckling.

"Good grief," said Tad. "I had no idea there was so much you could learn about the brain." He punched

Connor in the arm, although in all fairness, Connor had punched him first.

"It just points out how much there is to learn, period," said Aimi. "I don't think we will ever run out of things to learn."

"I think you're right, Aimi," agreed Grami. "In fact," she continued, "you five *LM Club* members already know more about how to talk to your brain—and to the brains of others—than most people on this planet."

"I know that I know a lot," said Stella. "I told myself that I could be a detective even if I am the littlest *LM Club* member. And here I am, a detective!" Stella clapped her hands, jumped up in the air, and twirled three times.

"Grami, do you have more examples of how to talk to your brain?" asked Toni.

"Well," said Grami, "neuroscientists have discovered that it's more effective to talk to yourself using your given name, the pronoun *you*, and positive instructions as if what you want it to do is already a done deal. For example, Stella could say: 'Stella, *you* are a detective. *You* can do research even if you're the littlest *LM Club* member.' It's like you and your brain are having a conversation."

"Stella, *you* are a detective. *You* can do research even if you're the littlest *LM Club* member," repeated Stella. "I can do that." Everyone clapped.

"Stella, *you* learn quickly," said Connor.

"Grami, *you* are a good teacher," said Aimi.

"Toni, *you* jazzercise very well," said Stella.

"Thoughts make your mindset, which creates your self-talk, that triggers your behaviors," said Tad. "Wow!"

"Remember, thoughts are just thoughts and you have the power to change them," said Grami. "Humans have a unique advantage over other creatures on this planet. Our brains allow us to make conscious choices about what we think and what we say and what we do, rather than just following reflexive reactions. You can change the way you feel by changing your thoughts. We can do that—if we choose to do so."

"Do you do that?" asked Connor. "Choose to change your thoughts?"

"I am learning to do that, Connor," said Grami. "I monitor whether I feel mad, scared, sad, or happy. When I identify a negative thought, I remind myself that I have the power to change my thoughts. If think, 'I can't do that,' I talk back to my brain. Kindly, of course."

"How would I do that?" asked Stella. "What would I say? I have to write a verse for school. Four lines, you understand, and they have to rhyme. I want to *know*."

"Be specific," said Grami. "Say, 'Stella, you are writing a four-line verse that rhymes and it is fun.'"

"There is a lot to learn," said Stella, sighing. "Have you learned everything yet, Grami?"

"I will be learning my whole life," said Grami.

"And since you are aiming to live to be a centenarian or a supercentenarian, Grami," said Toni, "you can learn a lot!"

"It's time to pack up the leftovers and leave for home," announced Grami. "Not that there are many leftovers," she added, smiling. "Five detectives, their club sponsor, and the *Longevity Mystery Club* mascot made sure of that."

Aimi and Stella held hands as they walked toward the car. Buddy-the-Beagle trotted along beside Stella. Toni walked beside Grami. Tad carried the empty brown wicker basket while Connor toted the empty water jug. At the car, they put the empty brown wicker basket and the empty water jug in the trunk. Then they all climbed into the car and fastened their seatbelts. Grami started the engine and drove toward home.

"Thank you for another adventure today, Grami," said Stella, yawning. Buddy-the-Beagle yawned, too. "When we get home, Buddy-the-Beagle and I are going to take a nap."

"Me, too," said Grami. "I laughed so hard today out there in the fresh air that I'm all relaxed."

"I have a book to read," said Toni. "I'll relax by reading my book."

"Connor and I will check on my rabbits," said Tad.

"Yeah," said Connor, laughing. "We'll see how many more kits they gave you, Tad. I don't even want to imagine how many rabbits you will have if you are a centenarian, much less a supercentenarian!" That comment make everyone laugh.

"I think I will relax by composing more on the *LM Club* song," said Aimi. "I really enjoy doing that."

And that's exactly what they did.

Your self-talk can help you win or lose,
So it is important what you choose.
At times, by helping another succeed,
You both reap benefits from that good deed.

3—Riddle Rescue

"Will someone please see who is at the front door?" called Grami. "I'm still clearing off my desk."

"I'll do it!" cried Stella, walking quickly down the hall. She *loved* answering the front door. It made her feel very grown-up and quite important. "Oh. Hello, Connor. It's you," she said. "What are you doing here at this time of the morning? And who is that man with you? And what is in the big box? I want to *know*."

"That's a lot of questions," said the man.

"Meet Jason," said Connor. "Grami's new computer is in the big box. We're going to set it up for her."

"Computer?" shouted Stella. She was so excited she clapped her hands, jumped up in the air, and twirled three times. "Aimi! Aimi!" she called, running back down the hall. "Grami has a new computer! Where *are* you?"

"Well, this is a fine howdy-do," said Jason, chuckling. "That girl just ran off and left us standing on the porch at the front door, computer and all."

"No worries," said Connor. "I know exactly where Grami wants her new computer. Follow me."

Grami was just removing the last book from her desk when Connor, Jason, and the big box appeared in her study. Stella and Aimi were right behind them.

"*When* did you buy a computer?" asked Stella. "I want to *know.*

"I bought it yesterday," said Grami, laughing.

"Oh, this is so exciting!" exclaimed Aimi, smiling.

"Last time we were at the Neo-Leo Wordpark, I learned that Internet searches are an age-proofing strategy and very good for the brain," Grami explained. "So I bought one."

"A *computer*," said Connor, seriously. "Grami already has a brain—a very good brain." Jason laughed out loud.

"I am very serious about a longevity lifestyle," said Grami, "and now I can look up brain and health information at home. I found a website with a BMI calculator: www.LongevityLifestyleMatters.com. That will be handy—for all of us, actually."

"BM," said Stella. "Did you say BM? I want to *know*."

"BMI," said Connor, laughing. "Grami said BMI, Stella. There's a big difference. BMI stands for Body Mass Index. It's all the rage for helping people get healthier. We can check our BMI scores on Grami's computer, too." Jason and Connor were carefully removing the computer from its box when Grami's shiny blue mobile rang.

"Will someone please answer that call for me?" asked Grami. "I'm helping Jason and Connor."

"I will," cried Stella. She *loved* answering the phone. It made her feel very grown-up and quite important. "Hello, this is Stella, a sleuth in the *Longevity Mystery Club*. May I help you?" She listened for a moment. "Oh. It's you. I'm answering her phone because Jason and Connor are helping Grami hook up her new computer." Pause. "You need to talk to her yourself? But why? I want to *know!*" Pause. "Oh, okay." Stella sighed as she handed the shiny blue mobile to Grami. "It's Tad."

"Hello, Tad," said Grami. She listened carefully and then said, "Yes. I think that's a good idea, and it will make a great adventure. We'll leave today at two o'clock sharp. Yes, I'll keep it a secret 'til you tell them."

Aimi asked, "Are we *all* going on an adventure?"

Grami nodded.

"Can Buddy-the-Beagle go with us?" asked Stella. "I want to *know.*"

Grami shook her head.

"Then it's a good thing I didn't promise him that he could come on this adventure," Stella said, sighing.

"You just heard about this adventure," said Connor. "So there was nothing *to* promise."

"I know," said Stella, giggling.

"Will there be something to research?" asked Aimi in her soft sweet voice. "I like being a flatfoot."

"There may be," said Grami. "This adventure is a secret until Tad tells you. We leave at two o'clock."

Two o'clock sharp found five *LM Club* members driving away in their sponsor's car. The *LM Club* mascot was at home on the screened-in back porch—with a treat.

"Okay, Tad," said Aimi. "What is the adventure? We've waited very patiently."

We're going to my first Riddle-Bee," said Tad, excitedly. "And I can hardly wait!"

"A Riddle-Bee?" asked Connor. "What's that? I've never heard of one before."

"It's a little like a Spelling-Bee except contestants use riddles," began Tad, "and then the ..."

"What are con-test-ants?" interrupted Stella. "Are we going to an ant farm? I want to *know*."

"No ant farm," said Grami. "Just listen, Stella."

Stella stopped talking and listened.

"A *contestant* is someone who participates in some type of competition," said Tad. "As I started to explain, a Riddle-Bee is a little like a Spelling-Bee. Each contestant says a riddle, and the moderator counts the number of seconds until someone in the audience solves the riddle correctly. The contestant whose riddle takes the longest number of seconds to solve, wins. I like riddles, and I've wanted to be in a Riddle-Bee for a long time."

"What riddle are you going to use?" asked Stella. "I want to *know*."

"Hopefully, a riddle for which you do not know the answer," said Tad, laughing. "I want a riddle that takes a very long time for the audience to solve."

"Maybe they won't solve it at all," suggested Aimi.

"Obviously, that would be very good," said Connor. "Then Tad would win the Riddle-Bee."

"Will lots of people be there?" asked Toni. "You don't like crowds."

"I don't know how many people will be there, Sis," Tad replied. "But I don't mind being on stage in front of a crowd. Then it's just like there are two of us: me and the audience. That's much easier than being *in* a large crowd of people with lots of noise and stuff going on. Sometimes when that happens I can hardly think!"

"I like crowds!" exclaimed Stella. "It's exciting!"

Grami chuckled. "That's one way you and Tad are different," she said. "Every brain is unique, you know."

Stella nodded her head vigorously, which made her curly ponytail bounce up and down and up and down. Fortunately, Stella's seatbelt held *her* firmly in place.

Once at the venue they saw a huge white tent that had been pitched in the middle of a soccer field. "Go get your seats," Tad suggested. "I'll sign in and pay the fee."

"We'll save you a seat," said Aimi.

Tad got in line to pay the one dollar registration fee. A red-headed, freckle-faced boy was in front of him. *Hmm-m,* Tad thought to himself. *That contestant doesn't look like he feels very well.* Once through the registration line, a volunteer escorted Tad to a roped-off area behind the raised wooden stage. Tad saw the same red-headed, freckled-faced boy leaning over a large garbage can, making some very unpleasant noises.

Tad walked over and said in a low voice, "Hey, man. Are you okay? My name is Tad."

"Not to worry. It's nothing catching," said the boy, looking up. "I'm Joel and this is my tenth Riddle-Bee— and I *always* throw up beforehand."

"Yikes," said Tad, sympathetically. "You do? This is my first Riddle-Bee. I would not like to upchuck."

"Who would?" asked Joel, grimacing. "I know I don't, but that doesn't stop it from happening."

"Hmm-m," said Tad. "Any idea what makes you upchuck?"

"I don't know," said Joel, shrugging his shoulders. "Probably just nerves. I love riddles and yet I'm terrified of competition." He shook his head sadly. "My dad says that's a paradox. You know, a statement that seems to say opposite things, both of which are also true. I got to hand it to my dad. He does try to encourage me. He says: *Don't be scared, Joel, don't forget your riddles, and don't throw up.'* I repeat those words over and over."

"Does it help?" asked Tad.

Joel shook his head. "I *wish*! But I still get scared, often forget my riddles, and *always* throw up. Naturally, the first thing I look for at a Riddle-Bee is the location of the nearest garbage can!"

"That's unfortunate," said Tad, sympathetically.

"Ya *think*?" asked Joel, managing a small smile. "In my case, I think it's *most* unfortunate."

Tad stood very still for a few moments, his brow furrowed. Finally, he asked, "I say, do you know about the *white bear* phenomenon?"

Joel looked puzzled. "The what?"

"The *white bear* phenomenon," repeated Tad.

Joel thought for a moment and then shook his red-haired head. "Nope, don't think so. *Should* I know?"

"No *shoulds* here," said Tad. "If you don't know, you don't know. But you can learn."

"Learn *what*?" asked Joel. "You're talking in riddles, but I'm all ears. Do tell, because I like riddles."

"When I say, 'Don't think about the white bear,' what do you see in your mind's eye?" asked Tad.

"Duh," said Joel. "That's doesn't take a rocket scientist. I picture a white bear, of course."

Tad nodded. "When you repeat those words, what do you see in your mind's eye?"

Joel was quiet for a few moments, then clapped his hand to his forehead, exclaiming: "Oh, my goodness. I see myself terrified out of my mind. Petrified, actually. Forgetting my riddles, sick to my stomach, and throwing up. Ridiculous! Dumb, even!

"Grami says you only know what you know," said Tad. "It's what you *don't* know you don't know that can give you the most trouble. She taught me a better way to talk to myself, one that helps me be more successful. She calls it positive self-talk."

"Positive self-talk?" asked Joel. "Listen, Tad, this is my tenth Riddle-Bee for heaven's sake, and I've never even placed. But I *always* throw up. Tell me what to say and be quick about it! We don't have much time."

"Your brain can only do what it thinks it can do," said Tad, "and it's your job to tell it what it can do. Use your given name so your brain knows who you are talking about, the pronoun 'you' and positive words only. Tell your brain what you want it to do as if it's a done deal. Stop talking about what you do not want to have happen."

Joel's face wrinkled in puzzlement. "Run that by me one more time," he said.

Tad did so. "Say it like this: 'Joel, you love Riddle-Bees. You remember your riddles. You feel good. You are having fun!'"

Quickly Joel repeated Tad's exact words, adding, "It seems a little weird, talking to my own brain that way. But, hey, it's a good kind of weird. I rather like it." He said the words again.

Suddenly Tad had a brain wave—a real genuine brainstorm. "Joel," he exclaimed, "listen up and pay attention. I'm giving you my best riddle."

The red-haired, freckle-faced boy looked a bit startled, but he listened carefully. Tad only had time to repeat the riddle twice before the moderator asked all contestants to come up on the raised wooden stage.

Tad punched Joel in the arm and whispered: "Joel, *you* are having *fun*." Joel punched him back and then both boys climbed the four steps up to the stage.

The first Riddle-Bee contestant said: "A blue house is made of blue bricks. A yellow house is made of yellow bricks. A red house is made of red bricks. An orange house is made of orange bricks. What is a *green* house made of?"

The moderator began to count off the seconds. One, two … At the end of five seconds, someone in the audience called out: "Glass. A greenhouse is made of glass."

Joel looked at Tad and winked. Tad winked back.

The next Riddle-Bee contestant said: "A customer purchased a $10,000 dollar car, but he didn't pay a single penny for it. How is that possible?"

This time it took eleven seconds before an audience member said, "Oh! Of course! He paid $10,000 *dollars*. Not a single **penny**."

The contestant with the five-second riddle sat down since eleven is more than five. "Oh, Grami," Aimi whispered. "I do so want Tad to do well. I want him to win!"

"I expect he'll do well," said Grami. "But remember, this is his first Riddle-Bee. He'll learn a great deal by participating in today's competition."

Several more contestants recited their riddles. All were solved by the audience in less than eleven seconds. Finally, Tad and Joel were the only contestants left.

Tad said: "I am the longest word in the English language that can be typed using letters that are all on the same line of keys. What am I?" The moderator counted out twelve seconds, thirteen seconds, fourteen seconds... An audience member shouted: *"Typewriter!"* Tad nodded.

"Fourteen seconds. That's the longest time, so far," said the moderator. The contestant with the eleven-second riddle sat down, because fourteen is more than eleven. "All right, young man," the moderator said, turning to Joel. "Let's have your riddle."

In a steady voice Joel repeated the riddle that Tad had given to him. The moderator again counted aloud. "Fourteen seconds. Fifteen seconds." Silence. "Fifteen seconds makes Joel the winner of this Riddle-Bee," said the moderator. "Congratulations, young man." The audience clapped and a few people whistled.

As they left the stage, Joel whispered to Tad, "That was your riddle. If you had used it, you'd have won. What made you give it to me?"

"Just a random act of kindness," replied Tad. "I'll be doing more of these Riddle-Bee's. But this is your tenth, and you'd never even placed before today. I had a hunch you might win with it. I'm happy for you!"

"Joel! Joel!" a man's voice shouted. "You did it! You did it! But how in the world did you do it, my boy?"

"Hi, Dad," said Joel, as the man came running up to the two boys. "Dad, this is Tad. He helped me win."

"He *what?*" asked Joel's father.

"He helped me win," repeated Joel, "by sharing the *white bear* phenomenon. I was talking to my brain in an unhelpful way. Explain it to him, Tad," said Joel.

"Oh, my goodness," said Joel's father, shaking his 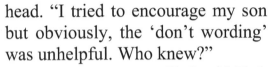 head. "I tried to encourage my son but obviously, the 'don't wording' was unhelpful. Who knew?"

"Not to worry, Sir," said Tad. "Grami says you only know what you know, and often it's what you don't know you don't know trips you up. No one can know everything—but Grami says 'Fortunately, you can choose to keep learning your whole life.'"

"I like the sound of your Grami," said the man, smiling. "Joel," he said, looking at this son, "I don't recall hearing that riddle before. Where did you get it? No one solved it, you know. "

"I know," said Joel, and then explained about Tad giving away his riddle. Joel's father listened, a stunned expression on his face. Finally, turning to Tad, the man asked, "Where did *you* get the riddle, son? Did you create it?"

"No, Sir," said Tad. "I didn't. I found it in the Book of Job. That's in the Old Testament, you know."

Joel's father did not look as if he had known that.

"Say, Tad, when were you planning to tell me the answer to the riddle?" asked Joel.

"The *answer*?" interrupted his father. "Joel, do you mean to tell me that you won this Riddle-Bee using something Tad gave you, and you don't even know the answer to the winning riddle? I can't believe it!"

"Yes and no," said Joel, laughing. "I only had time to hear the riddle twice before we were called onto the stage, and there was no time to get around to the answer. So 'yes' I won using something Tad gave me, and 'no' I don't know the answer to that riddle."

Joel's father whistled and shook his head. "Well, young man," he said to Tad, "what's the answer?"

"The answer, Sir, is a whale," said Tad.

"Well I never! If that doesn't beat all," said Joel's father. "We owe you, young man," and he stretched out an arm to shake Tad's hand. "You know, I had about decided to try talking Joel into quitting these Riddle-Bees after today, even though I know he loves riddles. Imagine, Joel

 finally won a Riddle-Bee—after his tenth try—using a riddle from another contestant, from a story that's thousands of years old, and without even knowing the answer. This is definitely one for the record books. It fairly blows my mind, it does!" The three laughed heartily. Handing a business card to Tad, Joel's father added, "Here is my contact information, young man. I hope you two can spend some time together creating riddles. See you around."

Turning to leave, Joel punched Tad in the arm, who promptly returned the gesture.

Smiling, Tad watched the two walk away, the father's arm slung over his son's shoulder.

"Tad! Tad! Over here!" Recognizing the voice as belonging to that of his twin sister, Tad turned toward the sound and saw Toni waving her arms wildly in the air.

Running to meet her, Tad was rewarded with a big hug and a kiss on each cheek. "This way," said Toni. "We saved a seat for you but didn't realize you'd be next to the last contestant."

"Well done, Tad," said Grami, when he had joined the group. "I'm proud of you. I think your brain enjoyed your first Riddle-Bee experience."

"You are so right," said Tad, enthusiastically. "My brain loved it. I can hardly wait to enter another one."

"But I wanted you to WIN!" said Stella. "I'm so-o-o-o-o disappointed, I *really* am. Why didn't you win? I want to *know*!"

Tad looked at the littlest detective. "I did win, Stella," said Tad, calmly, "so you can stop being *really* disappointed. Matter of fact, I think the Emotional Intelligence skills that Grami taught us helped me win in several ways. Four, to be exact."

"That's not how I figure it," Stella said. "It looks to me like you *lost*. How did your EQ skills help you *win* in *four* ways? I want to *know*."

"I'll list them for you," replied Tad, smiling. *"First,* I got to do something today that I've wanted to try for a long time. And I had fun doing it. *Second,* I met Joel, and I think we're going to be good friends—probably competitors, too. *Third,* because Grami taught us about the white bear phenomenon and self-talk, I was able to share that with Joel and he was able to apply it right then and there." Tad explained what had happened in the roped-off contestant area.

"You actually gave away your riddle?" asked Aimi in astonishment. "The winning riddle? I can't believe it. You'd have won if you'd used that riddle!"

"But that's only *three* wins," said Stella, interrupting. "You said you had *four* wins."

"I'm getting to that," said Tad, patiently. "My random act of kindness was my *fourth* win, and I'm happy with my choice. This was his tenth Riddle-Bee and he'd never even placed before. What I shared with Joel changed his life—and he's a fast learner. This was my first Riddle-Bee and I came in second. There's plenty of time for me to come in first. The way things turned out today is good."

"Right on," said Connor. "I agree with you, Tad. After all, the Vice-President is second only to the President." Grami and four members of the *LM Club* clapped.

"I suppose you're right," said Stella, albeit a little uncertainly. "And I am proud of you, too, even if you came in second." Tad laughed and laughed.

"I'm paying more attention to my self-talk now," said Aimi, as they walked toward the parking lot. "I've realized that I often talk to myself very negatively."

The five *LM Club* members and their sponsor got into the car and buckled up. Grami backed out of the parking space and drove out onto the highway.

"When someone criticizes me and says I didn't do a good job, I feel bad and tell myself I messed up," said Toni, as they rode toward home. "What can I do, Grami? I want to know more about self-talk."

"First, be very clear that those comments reflect another brain's opinion," said Grami. "It may be a valid observation, or it may simply reflect some jealousy on the part of that person." Toni nodded. "Second," continued Grami, "understand that you have a choice: you can blindly believe what every critic says or evaluate the comments for what you may be able to learn from them."

"But suppose they were right?" asked Toni.

"Sometimes a good critic can help you identify ways to improve," said Grami. "Analyzing your behavior and then deciding if you want to repeat it or tweak it or delete it is different from putting yourself down for making a mistake and then feeling bad. Everyone makes mistakes. That just reminds you that you're human. Ask yourself: 'Toni, is there something you can learn here?' If no, let it go. If yes, use what you learn to help you be more successful next time. Remember, tell your brain what you want to have happen as if it's already a done deal. Dump negative self-talk. You can be a victim or a survivor. It's up to you."

"Grami, what do you do when you hear negative self-talk in your head?" asked Aimi.

"I say: 'Grami, there's that negative thought again.' Then I change the negative thought into a positive one and usually repeat it aloud. I say, 'Grami, you are living a Longevity Lifestyle. You feel good.' An affirming self-talk style is a learned skill, you know. And you can choose to learn that skill. Here's a metaphor that I use," Grami continued. "I imagine that each day is like a whole pie. I ask myself: If a slice of pie represented the sum total of all my positive self-talk today, what would it look like? Would it be a big slice or just a tiny sliver? I'm aiming for bigger and bigger slices. Metaphorically, that is." Grami smiled.

"Great idea," said Connor. "You know how I enjoy metaphors!"

"Especially the *pie* part," said Tad, laughing. "And speaking of positive self-talk, would it be positive to tell our sponsor that I am very hungry and already enjoying the good meal—in my mind's eye—that Grami prepared?"

"It would be both positive and true," said Grami. "Your *LM Club* sponsor planned ahead and a big pot of black bean chili and three dozen honey-corn muffins are waiting at home. Plenty of peanut butter, too."

"That's six muffins apiece," said Connor. "Great!"

"Let's practice saying positive things while we drive home," said Toni.

"I'll start," said Tad. "Thank you, Grami. We sure lucked out when you agreed to be our club sponsor."

"We can say positive things as we ride in the car and positive things as we eat that good meal of black bean chili and corn muffins," said Aimi.

And that's exactly what they did.

A turtle named Tikki agreed to a race,

With a feisty hare who set a fast pace.

But the hare was cocky and took a nap,

Losing the race on the very last lap.

4—Double Jeopardy

"Grami, I brought you something," said Toni.

"Why, thank you," said Grami, smiling as she opened the tiny package. "Great! I'll use this measuring tape every week when I take measurements."

"Measurements? What measurements?" asked Stella. "I want to *know*."

"Each week I measure my waist, calculate my BMI, check my weight, complete my Daily Goals form, and write down the data," said Grami, pointing to forms pinned to the cork board above her new computer.

Toni looked at Grami's Weekly Measurement Form. "Weeks one and two your weight was 160 pounds (72.5 kilograms)," said Toni, "Week three it was 158 pounds (71.7 kilograms). Grami, you lost some weight!"

"That's my goal," said Grami, smiling.

"But your BMI is still 31," said Stella.

"It will take a while for my BMI to move out of the obese category," said Grami. "But it will happen."

"I want you to live to be a supercentenarian," said Stella, seriously.

"So do I," said Grami, smiling. "After you formed the *Longevity Mystery Club*, I developed a plan I call "Longevity Lifestyle," one that I will follow for as long as I live."

"How much should you weigh, Grami?" asked Tad. "If you don't mind my asking, that is."

"According to the doctor," said Grami, "my weight needs to be in the range of 135 pounds, or 61 kilograms."

"Hmm-m," said Aimi. "That's 24 pounds or 10.8 kilograms *less* than your weight right now."

"That's right. You are good at math," said Grami, nodding. "As my life gets back into better balance, so will my weight."

"Your waist was 36.5 inches or 93 centimeters," said Toni, still looking at the Measurement Form.

"I know," said Grami. "And I also know it needs to be 35 inches or 90 centimeters—or less. Slowly and surely that is happening, too. Remember, I started this journey

with a waist that was well over 37 inches or 94 centimeters. Already my clothes are a little bit looser. That's a great feeling!"

"And what are the waist measurements for men?" asked Connor.

"The internet said 40 inches (101 centimeters) or less," said Grami.

Connor and Tad looked at each other. "Our waist measurements are way under that," said Connor.

"I plan to keep it that way," said Tad. "I want a Daily Goals form like yours, Grami. Will you give us copies of your form?"

"Of course I will," said Grami, nodding.

"You don't need to lose weight, Tad," said Toni.

"Neither do you, Toni," said her twin brother.

"A Longevity Lifestyle isn't about losing weight unless you are overweight or obese," said Grami. "It is about finding your optimum weight and staying there. In my case, that's about 135 pounds or 61 kilograms."

"Are you still going to fix us lunch when we have *LM Club* meetings?" asked Tad.

"Certainly," said Grami. "After all, I'm the *Club* sponsor. Maybe that's something you five detectives will investigate. You can help me plan healthier meals."

"Sure," said Tad, "but this week we're researching exercise. Physical and mental exercise."

"Exercise is one of your goals, Grami," said Toni.

"Twenty minutes of physical exercise every day," said Grami. "I started at ten minutes. Now I'm up to twenty minutes, and eventually I'll increase to thirty minutes. I've been walking first thing each morning because I read that exercise before breakfast helps my body turn on fat-burning peptides or chemicals that last for several hours. And I'm eating a nutritious breakfast every day, too, including some healthier complex carbs."

"That stands for carbohydrates, Stella," said Aimi, before Stella could ask the question.

"Heathier carbs like old-fashioned oats and avocado on baked crackers or sourdough bread are good brain fuels," said Grami. "A good breakfast boots up my brain."

"At least one serving of fruit every day and two servings of vegetables," Connor read. "That's not hard to do. And six to eight hours of sleep each night."

"I did an Internet search about sleep and was amazed to learn that sleep is independently linked with longevity," said Grami. "I now go to bed by ten o'clock every night and usually sleep until six or seven in the morning. Oh, and I've started sleeping on my side because studies have shown a side position seems to improve the removal of waste products from the brain. My new computer is turning out to be real handy!"

"It's real handy for us, too," said Aimi, smiling.

"You've done a lot of research on your new computer," said Tad. "I heard that volunteer at the Neo-Leo Wordpark tell you that learning to use a computer and do Internet searches is an anti-aging strategy because it stimulates the brain. That's especially important for older persons."

"Are you an older person, Grami?" asked Stella. "I want to *know*."

"I am an older person," said Grami. "And this older person—for one—is aiming to live to at least 122 years 164 days. Maybe 165 days. I'm on my way!"

"I like this list," said Toni, looking at Tad. "I want to make a Daily Goals form for me, too."

"I can't read your writing," said Tad to Grami. "What does this next goal say?"

"Mental exercises for thirty minutes every day," said Grami. "That was my own add-on goal. I want to keep my brain sharp. I like brain benders, riddles, word games, and puzzles.

"Riddles," said Tad. "Writing riddles is going to be on my list for mental stimulation. That's going to be so much ..." The ringing telephone interrupted Tad.

Grami answered her bright blue mobile. The five *LM Club* members heard her say, "Hello. Yes. How are you? . . . Oh, my! That's too bad. . . . I understand. What are you going to do?. . . I see. Well, that's a good idea. . . . Her dog? Oh, well, the five *LM Club* detectives are all right here. I'll ask them and call you back."

"Who was on the phone?" asked Aimi. "That sounded like a mysterious conversation."

"And what is too bad?" asked Tad.

"And what do you want to ask us detectives?" asked Stella. "I want to *know*."

"That was Marcia," said Grami, answering Aimi's question first. "You know that her mother lives in the tiny cottage that sits partway up the bank overlooking the lake. Sadly, she tripped on the steps and fell."

"Marcia?" asked Toni.

"No, Marcia's mother," said Grami. "The paramedics came and took her to the Hospital's Emergency Department. She broke her left leg in two places and is in surgery right now. She will be in the hospital for some time."

"What was that about her dog?" asked Connor. "I'm with Stella on this one. I what to know what you said you'd ask the *LM Club* members."

"I'll tell you right now," said Grami. "I was just coming to that. Marcia wants to know if we will go over to her mother's tiny cottage, put out the garbage bins, feed the dog, and then give it a run on the sand by the water's edge. Marcia will come and pick up the dog tomorrow and keep it until her mother returns home."

"I fell off the huge jungle gym at the park," said Aimi softly, remembering, "and Grami took me to the Hospital's Emergency Department, so I know what that's like. I didn't have to stay in the hospital, but I did have a pink cast on my arm."

"And we all signed our names on your pink cast," said Toni.

"I'd like to help," said Tad, quickly. "I like to do random acts of kindness."

"Me, too," said Connor.

"Count me in," said Toni.

"Buddy-the-Beagle and I want to go," said Stella. "See, Buddy-the-Beagle is sitting there with his *I-want-to-go* smile. Please say he can come, Grami. And do I need to bring *My Sleuth Notebook*?"

"Yes and no," said Grami, chuckling. "Yes, he will enjoy a run on the sand beside the lake. And no, you will not need your *Notebook*."

"Call Marcia and tell her that the members of the *LM Club*—plus the sponsor and mascot—are on their way," said Stella. She was so excited she clapped her hands, jumped up in the air, and twirled three times.

Grami called Marcia back on her shiny blue mobile. Then they got into Grami's car and drove to the tiny cottage. After Grami parked the car in the driveway, they walked toward the back door of the tiny cottage that sat partway up the bank overlooking the lake.

"What is that sound?" asked Aimi. "Listen. There it is again. What *is* it?"

"It sounds like a dog howling," said Connor. At that, Buddy-the-Beagle threw back his head, pointed his little nose in the air, opened his little mouth, and began to howl.

"That's quite a doggie duet," said Grami, laughing.

"Hold it," said Connor excitedly. "That sounds like a New Guinea Singing Dog."

"A New Guinea what?" asked Tad.

"A New Guinea Singing Dog," said Connor. "It's one of the rarest dogs in the world. I'll know for sure when we get inside, and I can take a look at it."

Grami opened the back door to the tiny cottage and everyone crowded around to peek inside. Buddy-the-Beagle stuck his little nose around the corner. There, sitting forlornly in the center of a round braided rug, was a small light brown dog. It had a rather wide head set with almond-shaped, dark-amber eyes. The tip of its tail and all four paws were white. There was a small white patch on its face and one on its little chest.

"I knew it," said Connor. "I knew it sounded like a New Guinea Singing Dog. And now I see that it looks like the New Guinea Singing Dog, too. I saw one on YouTube."

Connor walked over and knelt down on the rug beside the small light brown dog. It licked Connor's hand. "As I live and breathe," whispered Connor, "this is the first live New Guinea Singing Dog I've ever seen, other than in a picture. In real life, I mean."

"The dog may be thirsty," said Grami. "See if you can find a water bowl, Stella."

Stella did and the small light brown dog was. Thirsty, that is. So was Buddy-the-Beagle. While Buddy-the-Beagle and the small light brown dog quenched their thirst and got acquainted with each other, Connor and Tad set out the garbage bins as Marcia had requested. It was an easy job for the two boys.

"I don't believe I've ever even heard of a New Guinea Singing Dog," said Grami. "What do you know about them, Connor?"

"As I mentioned earlier," said Connor, "I saw a YouTube program about them. I'll tell you what I know, and you can be sure that I'll be doing some more sleuthing about them at our next visit to the Neo-Leo Wordpark."

"Or on Grami's computer," said Aimi.

Connor nodded and continued. "They are genuine wild dogs that were discovered in New Guinea in the 1950s. A long neck allows them to toss their head three hundred and sixty degrees. They may live to be twenty years old. Nicknamed *singers*, when a group of them get together, each dog can howl a single note in a slightly different pitch from the others, which makes for an unusual sound."

"Very interesting, Connor," said Grami. "I learned something new today."

The members of the *LM Club* and their sponsor— plus *two*—left the tiny cottage and walked down the path toward the hard-packed sand that bordered the edge of the lake. Well, some of them walked. Two ran, side by side, their tails wagging furiously.

"I wonder what Marcia's mother named this New Guinea Singing Dog," said Stella. "I want to *know*."

"Oh, I forgot to tell you!" said Grami. "It's Diva."

"Divas are often singers," said Connor. "That's a good name for this dog."

"My music teacher said *Diva* means *princess* in Latin," said Toni. "I agree. It is a good name for this little *singer*."

"The word *Diva* can also be used to denote a woman of outstanding talent in almost any area," added Grami.

"I want to be a woman of outstanding talent," said Stella.

"You likely will be," said Grami, chuckling.

"Look at Buddy-the-Beagle and Diva-the-Princess run," said Aimi. "They are just tearing up the sand. I'm

57

glad they are playing and having fun." They watched Buddy-the-Beagle and Diva-the-Singer run back and forth and back and forth on the hard-packed sand along the water's edge.

After a while Connor said, "Let's race, Tad."

"I'd just like to run," said Tad. "Not race. Let's see if we can keep up with Buddy-the-Beagle and Diva-the-Singer." The two boys ran and ran. Eventually they turned around and came back to join the others.

"When I started walking every morning," said Grami, "I told myself 'Grami, you enjoy walking and you feel good.' And guess what? I do."

"Maybe you'll lose another pound," said Stella. "I could write that on your Weekly Measurement Form."

Grami laughed. "I would need to expend thirty-five hundred calories more than I take in to lose a pound, Stella. But I'm not focusing on losing weight, as I told you. Rather, I'm concentrating on creating a balanced brain-based Longevity Lifestyle that I'll maintain for the rest of my life. But exercise does strengthen your muscles and can help maintain your optimum weight when you do reach it."

"I read on the computer that too much sitting can put your health in jeopardy," said Toni.

"What is jep-ar-dy?" asked Stella. "I want to *know*."

"It comes from an old French expression, *jeu parti*," said Grami. "Literally it means *divided game* where the outcome is uncertain."

"So jeopardy means that you are in danger of losing something," said Aimi.

"In this case, your health," said Toni.

"Well," said Tad, "if not enough physical exercise puts your health at risk, then not enough mental exercise can put your brain at risk, too. And everything starts in your brain."

"That would be double jeopardy," said Connor.

"Clever," said Grami. "Double jeopardy."

"Riddles definitely start in my brain," said Tad. "In fact, my brain is thinking about a new riddle right now. I'll tell you as soon as my brain figures it out."

"I hope you lost another pound walking by the lake, Grami," said Stella. "I like things to happen quickly."

"I know you do, Stella," said Grami. "However, doing things quickly is not always the best choice."

"Why not?" asked Stella. "Why is doing things quickly not always the best choice? I want to *know*."

Let's sit down on this big log, and I'll tell you an old fable. There are several more logs close by so there is plenty of room for everyone."

"What's a fay-bull?" asked Stella. "Is there a bull named Fay? I want to *know*." At that, Tad and Connor started laughing so hard they could hardly catch their breath.

"Oh, Stella," said Aimi, sighing. "A fable is a type of story, like the tale of 'Goldilocks and the Three Bears,' or 'Snow White and the Seven Dwarfs.' Just listen, will you? My teacher said we have two ears and only one mouth, so we should listen twice as much as we talk."

"Oh," said Stella. "Okay. I am ready to listen."

As soon as the five *LM Club* members and Grami sat down, the two dogs stopped running up and down the hard-packed sand along the water's edge and plopped down beside the logs, a pink tongue lolled from the side of each panting mouth. When all were settled comfortably, Grami began:

Once upon a time, a long time ago, so the story goes, there was a hare...

"A hare? What is a hare?" Stella interrupted. "It can't be something that grows on your head because there are many more hairs than just one on a person's head. I want to *know*."

There was a moment of silence and then Tad said, "A hare is another name for

a rabbit, Stella. Would you start again, Grami?"

Grami nodded and began again.

Once upon a time, a long time ago, so the story goes, there was a hare who was overly impressed with how fast it could run. It also had a bad habit of teasing and ridiculing a turtle named Tikki for moving so abysmally slow, at the speed of, well, a turtle. Eventually Tikki the turtle got tired of being called a 'slow poke' and ridiculed for just plodding along—and surprised even himself by challenging the hare to a race. For its part the hare laughed and laughed and readily agreed to the race.

The appointed day came and the race began. No surprise, the hare soon left Tikki the turtle way behind, eating the hare's dust, no less. A little cocky because he was so-o-o-o supremely confident of winning, the hare decided to take a little nap midway through the agreed-

upon course. Settling himself comfortably in the shade of a nearby tree, the hare was soon fast asleep.

Eventually, Tikki the turtle came to a bend in the path and saw the hare snoozing under the tree. But the turtle did not stop. It just kept plodding along, slowly and steadily. Sometime later the hare, awakening from his siesta, discovered that Tikki the turtle was no longer in sight. The hare looked up the road and down the road, but it could not see the turtle. Anywhere. Putting on a burst of bunny speed, the supremely cocky hare sprinted for the finish line, his legs simply eating up the path.

To its astonishment and complete consternation, the supremely confident and cocky hare saw its competitor slowly and steadily crossing the finish line. The hare was too late and not the least bit amused. But it was a done deal. The race was over and the hare was 'toast,' as the old saying goes. Tikki the turtle, plodding steadily along, had won.

"The moral of that fable," said Grami, "is that slow and steady wins in the long run."

"You have rabbits, Tad," said Stella. "Could you find a turtle and have a turtle-hare race? I want to *know.*"

"I don't want a turtle-hare race," said Tad. "I do want to write a verse about that fable, though, as soon as I figure out my riddle . . . Oh, I think I've got it! What is both a mental *and* a physical exercise that contributes to health and longevity? Think of something unusual that happened today."

"Running on the beach?" asked Toni.

Tad shook his head.

"Putting out the garbage bins?" asked Stella.

"That's not unusual," said Tad, smiling.

"Something *unusual*," mused Connor. "I've got it," he shouted. "Doggie duets! It's singing!"

"Right," said Tad. And wouldn't you know? At that very moment both Buddy-the-Beagle and Diva-the-Singer threw back their heads, pointed their little noses in the air, opened their little mouths, and began to howl.

"Listen to that, will you," said Aimi. "They are singing a doggie-duet encore."

"They sound pretty good," said Grami. "Especially for not having ever practiced together before today's performance." Everyone laughed. Buddy-the-Beagle and Diva-the-Singer did not laugh. They just kept on singing and singing and singing or howling and howling and howling, depending on your point of view.

"I heard some Canadian singers on TV," said Aimi. "They were called The Four Tenors. Maybe we could call Buddy-the-Beagle and Diva-the-Singer 'Canine Duets."

"And if we filmed them singing their canine duets and put the recording on YouTube, they might become famous," said Connor.

When Grami finally stood up to go, Buddy-the-Beagle took one look at her and his half of the duet came to a sudden stop as he ran over to join Grami.

"Just look at that smart dog," said Tad, laughing. "He knows who has keys to the car. Grami."

They walked back to the tiny cottage that sat partway up the bank overlooking the lake. Stella gave each dog water to drink and made sure to leave food for Diva-the-Singer in her doggie dish.

"Today turned out to be a great adventure," said Connor, gazing dreamily out the window as Grami drove toward home. "An unexpected adventure. Who knew? I've heard New Guinea Singing Dogs on YouTube, but this is the first time I've ever seen and heard one in person."

"By agreeing to help Marcia, we all got to see our first New Guinea Singing Dog up close and personal," said Tad. He paused. "You know, I'm hungry. Listening to that doggie duet has made me very hungry."

"More likely it was your running on the beach that made you very hungry," said Toni, laughing.

"As soon as we get home, your *Longevity Mystery Club* sponsor—that's me—will fix lunch," said Grami.

"And I'll write down my riddle plus a verse about the turtle-hare race in *My Sleuth Notebook,*" said Tad.

"I'll set the table," said Toni.

"I'll fill a pitcher with water," said Connor.

"I'll feed Buddy-the-Beagle," said Stella.

"I'll pull radishes from our garden and wash them," said Aimi, smiling happily at Grami, who returned the smile.

"I'll put out six napkins," said Tad. "After that, my job will be to help make giant inroads into Grami's yummy lunch."

And that's exactly what they did.

The new adventure was really fun,
And all were sorry when it was done.
Each LM Club member had a good run,
Learning to balance—one by one.

5—Challenging Challenges

"Grami," said Aimi, irritation tingeing her usually soft sweet voice, "the antique grandfather clock is not working right—again. It goes tick-tock, tick-tock—then *rests* for a while. When it starts tick-tocking again, it's behind by several seconds. A few more *rests* and it's behind by a few minutes. Unhelpful in a clock!"

"Your candy red mobile phone has a built-in clock," said Tad. "Just saying."

"I know and I *could* use that," said Aimi, "but what's the point of having an antique grandfather clock if it doesn't keep good time? It's a regular predicament."

"More like an *irregular* predicament," said Toni. "It *is* nice to look at. That should count for something."

"Yes, it is," said Connor, "but I get Aimi's point. If you are depending on that antique time piece and it is inaccurate, you could miss something important."

"It's definitely an *irregular* predicament," said Grami, laughing. "I'll ask the clock-maker to send his assistant out to the house to rebalance the mechanism."

"I practiced my ukulele for five whole minutes longer than usual," said Stella. "I didn't realize that clock was taking a *rest* between its tick-tocking."

"That didn't hurt you," said Aimi, laughing.

"This irregular clock predicament is a metaphor for a less-than-healthy lifestyle," said Grami.

"I forgot what *met-a-four* means," said Stella.

"Look on my new computer," suggested Grami.

"Oh, right," said Stella. "I don't have to wait until we visit the Neo-Leo Wordpark again." She typed in a search. "It says *metaphor* is a word or phrase that is used to compare two people, things, animals, or places."

"I was like the antique grandfather clock—not working very well," said Grami. "My life was out of balance, and I gained a lot of weight. Now that I'm on a Longevity Lifestyle, my life is getting back in balance."

"That is so-o-o-o good," said Toni.

"Remember the DVD we watched at the Neo-Leo Wordpark?" asked Grami. The five members of the *Longevity Mystery Club* nodded. "It said that many children and adults drink *counterfeit* water—regular or diet sodas, fruit juices, and sugary drinks. Water is now my beverage of choice. No *counterfeit* water for me."

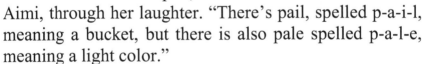

Stella looked at Grami's Daily Goals form. "What does 'pale urine' mean?" asked Stella. "Do you have to pee in a pail? I want to *know*."

"There are two English words that sound like pail," said Aimi, through her laughter. "There's pail, spelled p-a-i-l, meaning a bucket, but there is also pale spelled p-a-l-e, meaning a light color."

"Pale urine refers to pee that is almost clear in color," said Grami. "That goal is to help me avoid becoming dehydrated, which is not good for my brain or my body."

Stella started to open her mouth but Toni said quickly, "*Dehydrated* means that you've not been drinking enough water to replace what you lose through sweating, breathing, and waste products like urine."

"Oh," said Stella. "De-hi-dray-shun."

"I need to drink enough water, so I have at least one p-a-l-e urine every day," said Grami. "If it's a hot day I might need to drink even more water than usual. After all, I do not want to be a pee brain."

"Pee brain?" asked Tad. "What's a pee brain? I'm already quite sure I have no desire to be a pee brain and I don't even know what it is!"

"Good for you," said Grami, laughing. "You definitely want to avoid being a pee brain. Dehydration was on Toni's list of factors that can shorten one's longevity. I did an Internet search on my new computer and learned some very interesting information."

"What did you learn?" asked Stella. "I want to *know*."

"Hold your horses, hold your horses," said Grami.

"But I have no horses," said Stella. "I only have Buddy-the-Beagle and he's a dog, not a horse."

"Stella," said Aimi, laughing. "That's just an expression!"

"The expression, *hold your horses*, means you need to be patient," said Grami. "Give me a chance to tell you."

"But it's so-o-o-o hard for me to wait," Stella said, sighing loudly. "It's very hard indeed!"

"As I was saying," said Grami, smiling, "I learned that my brain is more than three-quarters water and needs a regular supply of fresh water each and every day. If I fail to drink enough, my brain might need to ask my bladder to send some fluid up to my brain. A rather unpleasant thought, that, as I have no desire to be a pee brain, either!"

"Yuck!" said Connor, grimacing. "I want pure water for my brain. Count me out."

"I'm with Tad and Connor," said Toni. "No pee brain for me!"

"Me either," said Aimi.

"Count me out of that business," said Stella. "I'm holding my horses, I am."

"The *LM Club* meets tomorrow, you know," said Toni. "Each *Club* member is going to make a Daily Goals form. We want to be healthy and balanced."

"That's a good idea," said Grami. "You'll probably have some items in common. But, since every brain is unique, some items may be different."

"I'm putting *one p-a-l-e urine a day* on my Daily Goals form," said Connor.

Mine, too," said Tad. "I bet that will be on everyone's Daily Goals form. As Toni said, we *LM Club* sleuths want to be healthy and balanced."

"Speaking of balance," said Grami, "your sponsor has planned an adventure for the *LM Club* members. We will leave at 10 o'clock tomorrow morning."

"After we have all eaten a good breakfast and finished our practicing," said Aimi.

"Oh, what fun!" cried Stella. "What is the adventure, Grami? I want to *know*."

"It's a secret," said Grami, smiling at Stella. And to her credit, Stella smiled back and did not ask again. She really was *holding her horses*. "Wear sturdy walking shoes and bring sun glasses and a jacket," added Grami.

Next morning, five LMC members climbed into Grami's car, buckled their seatbelts, and off they went. Thirty minutes later, Grami drove under a large wooden archway and parked the car. "Here we are," she said. "We've arrived at the Champion Challenge Course."

"What is a cham-pea-on chal-enj-kors?" asked Stella. "Is it about green peas? I want to *know*."

"Who can answer that?" asked Grami.

"Which word?" asked Tad.

"Your choice," Grami replied.

"*Champion*," said Tad, "means a person with such good skills that he or she is a winner—or could be a winner. A champion could also be an individual who

supports a cause, like the Red Cross or Special Olympics."

"I'll take the word *challenge*," said Connor. "A challenge is something that takes a great deal of effort and sometimes a lot of special skill. A challenge might be trying to improve your own performance or it could be competing against the skills of others as in extreme sports."

"Champion Challenge Course," said Connor. "Two words down and one to go."

"A *course* can mean more than one thing," said Toni. "It can mean a set of lessons as in school—but this doesn't look much like a school."

"That word can also mean a path or road or river rapids that *course* though a gorge or canyon," said Grami.

"I thought *coarse* meant rough," said Aimi.

"It does. But *coarse* meaning rough is spelled c-o-**a**-r-s-e. The other word *course* sounds the same but is *spelled c-o-**u**-r-s-e,*" explained Grami.

"I think I have a word headache," sighed Stella.

"A word headache would be a *challenge,* of *course,*" said Connor, laughing. "That's a third definition—meaning naturally or stating the obvious. It may be a headache for some, but words are fun for me."

"A *word* headache," said Aimi. "That's a new one, Stella. It reminds me of a student in our class who is just learning to speak English. It must be a *challenge,* of *course*"—Aimi paused while Connor laughed—"for someone who grew up speaking another language to learn English. Some words in English sound the same but have different meanings, like the number two, spelled t-w-o and the word too, spelled t-o-o, which means also."

"And some words are spelled the same but are pronounced differently and mean different things," said Connor. "The word *wind* is spelled w-i-n-d, meaning a breeze or a gale, and *wind,* that's spelled the same way but means to crank up or rev up something."

"That does it," said Stella, waving both arms in the air like a windmill. "That absolutely does it. Wind and wind. Two and too. Coarse and course. I don't just *think* I have a word headache, I absolutely *know* I have one!"

That triggered some chuckles.

"Grami," said Aimi thoughtfully, "how come you sometimes ask 'Who can answer that'? Don't you know the answer?"

"Although one person never knows everything," replied Grami, "often I *do* know the answer. Knowing something yourself is one thing, but being able to explain it to someone else is a horse of a different color. When you can describe it clearly to another person, you help them to understand it better. And you also reinforce it in your own brain. I ask because it's good practice for *LM Club* members."

"Horse of a different color," repeated Stella. "That's another something like 'hold your horses,' so it must be one of those *met-a-for thing-a-ma-jig-gies*."

Stella's comment hit Connor right smack-dab in the middle of his funny bone, and he began to laugh. Watching Connor, Tad also began to laugh, and soon both boys were doubled over. And because laughter is catching, soon all five *LM Club* members and their sponsor were laughing, too. Laughing to beat the band.

"Oh, Stella," said Grami, wiping tears from her eyes, "You learn fast and you are a regular little comedienne. I do so enjoy your sense of humor!"

When everyone had laughed themselves out, five *LM Club* members and their sponsor walked toward the entrance booth.

"You all wore sturdy walking shoes," said Grami.

"Well, you told us to do that," said Toni.

"But people don't always follow directions like they're supposed to," said Connor.

"The *LM Club* members did," said Tad. "Even Stella."

"Are you teasing me again?" asked Stella.

"Of course," said Tad, and then he and Connor started laughing all over again.

"The *LM Club* members do follow directions," said Grami. "It's a pleasure to be the *Club* sponsor."

"We always learn something on our adventures," said Aimi. "What are we here to learn? We may as well talk about it while Tad and Connor are laughing."

"I hope you *learn* that learning is fun," said Grami. Toni smiled and Aimi jumped up and down. Stella was so excited she clapped her hands, jumped up in the air, and twirled three times. Tad and Connor did not clap or jump or twirl. They were still laughing. Grami just smiled.

When they reached the entrance booth, a young man stepped forward and said, "Welcome to the Champion Challenge Course. My name is Guy. I will be your coach and guide today. Guy the guide."

Grami introduced herself and the five *LM Club* sleuths. "We are here to learn about balance," she said.

"Which, of course, is the reason you have chosen to visit the Champion Challenge Course," said Guy the guide. "Which course do you want today?"

"The balance course, of course," replied Grami promptly, "spelled *course* and not *coarse*."

"Good one, Grami," said Guy the guide. "Follow me down Equipoise Lane, the path that leads to the first challenge. *Equipoise* is another name for balance, you know. And you need balance in almost every area of life."

"Eck-wi-poys," said Stella, sounding out the word. "Another name for balance."

"That's another thing about English words," said Connor. "They sometimes sound different from the way they're spelled. Equipoise has the letter 'q' in it but it sounds like 'k.'"

"It also has the letter 'u' but it sounds like 'w' as in we," said Tad. "You're right, Connor. This word stuff is fun!'"

"My name sounds just like it is spelled," said Stella.

"Not exactly," said Aimi. "Your name has two l's.' It should be pronounced Stel-el-a."

"Ah, yes," said Guy the guide, chuckling. "The challenge of the English language. And here we are. The purpose of this *course*, spelled c-o-u-r-s-e, is to help you understand the importance of balance or *equipoise,* spelled *e-q-u-i-p-o-i-s-e*. The first activity on this balance course is right in front of you." He pointed to a long row of wooden pegs stuck in the ground about 12 inches or 30 centimeters apart. The top of each peg was flat and about the size of a salad plate. The pegs reached up to Stella's knee cap. "Step up on the first wooden peg and then walk along the row of pegs alternating your feet. Left, right, and so on."

One at a time, the *LM Club* members walked along the row of wooden pegs without stepping onto the ground.

"That was easy," said Tad.

"So far, so good," said Guy the guide. "Not everyone makes it to the end without stepping off."

"The *LM Club* members have good balance," said Aimi, and told Guy the guide about the *Longevity Mystery Club*, their sponsor, and their mascot.

"That sounds like fun," said Guy the guide. Pointing to a long narrow wooden plank that was about four inches or ten centimeters wide and about the length of a big banana off the ground, he said, "Here is your second activity. Step up onto the plank and walk to the end, putting one foot in front of the other. Each of you will do this exercise twice. The first time through, I want the rest of the group to call out: 'Don't fall! Don't fall!' We'll see if that improves your performance."

"I can do this," cried Stella, jumping up onto the wooden plank. But after just a few steps, Stella lost her balance and jumped down to the ground. "Oh my!" she exclaimed. "That's harder than it looks."

"Let me try," said Aimi. She made it half-way along the wooden plank and then began to wobble and stepped off. "Stop saying 'Don't fall!'" cried Aimi. "I saw pictures of falling in my mind's eye."

"That's exactly my point," said Guy the guide. "It's important what you say to yourself and what others say to you. Let's see how the rest of your group does."

Toni was the only one who walked the entire length of the plank without falling.

"Good job, Toni!" exclaimed Tad. "But *how* did you do it?"

"I told myself: 'Toni, you are walking on this wooden plank until you reach the end. Toni, put out your arms to help you balance.' And it worked!"

"Excellent," said Guy the guide. "Now, I want the peanut gallery to call out something different."

"What is a peanut gallery?" asked Stella. "Does it have anything to do with peanuts? I want to *know*."

"No," said Guy the guide. "It's a term for a group of people who are calling out instructions to others."

"Oh," said Stella. "It made me hungry for peanuts."

"This time, I want the peanut gallery to call out: 'Put out your arms. Stay balanced. You can do this,'" said Guy the guide.

Aimi stepped up onto the piece of wood. "I want you to talk to yourself, too, young lady," said Guy the guide. "Say: 'Aimi, you are walking successfully to the end.' And picture yourself doing it."

Aimi stayed up on the plank all the way to the end. "It's easier to do this when the peanut gallery says, 'Stay balanced. You can do this.' I saw myself doing just that in my mind's eye," said Aimi.

"Good," said Guy the guide. "Always tell your brain what you want to have happen. It sure helps to have friends who speak positively to you."

The second time, everyone walked to the end of the plank successfully. Even Stella.

"I told my brain, 'Stella, you walk to the end of the wooden plank.' And I did!" Everyone clapped for Stella, the littlest *LM Club* member. She was so excited she clapped her hands, jumped up in the air, and twirled three times. On the ground, of course, not up on the wooden plank.

The third balance exercise used square wooden posts driven into the ground. (A CD or DVD case would fit on the top of each post.) These posts were almost twice as high off the ground as the first wooden pegs and were about 18 inches apart or 48 centimeters apart. Toni went first. She stepped onto the first wooden post with her right foot. She moved her left foot to the second wooden post and then she just stood there. "My right foot wants to stay where it is," Toni said. "It looks so far to the third post."

"Shift your weight slightly as if you were standing on your left leg," said Guy the guide "Tell your brain: 'Toni, you look at the third post and move your right foot to it.' That way your brain knows what to do."

Toni did as the Guy the guide suggested. "I did it," cried Toni.

"Yes, you did," said Guy the guide. "Now do the same thing all over again using your left foot."

"But you helped me," said Toni.

"I gave you suggestions," said Guy the guide. "I offered you coaching. You could have chosen not to follow my suggestions. However, you and your brain followed my suggestions and then did the work."

"And I was successful," said Toni, smiling happily. Guy the guide walked right beside Toni until she reached the end of the posts successfully.

"Now, the rest of you each take a turn," said Guy the guide. This time Stella went last. She stepped up on the first block with her right foot and put her left foot on the second block of wood. It was a stretch. A long stretch. "Maybe I'm too little to do this," said Stella. "I couldn't reach the cross-bar for the new Red Roller ride at the Turvy-Topsy Amusement Park, either."

"Not so fast," said Guy the guide. "Avoid jumping to conclusions, Stella. Sometimes we need some help from others. It's called collaboration."

"Co-lab-o-ray-shun," said Stella. "I know what that word means. It's a joint venture like when we collaborated at Kamp Kona to build a humongous sand castle."

"How can collaboration help Stella on this balance activity?" asked Toni.

"Let me show you," said Guy the guide. "Toni, stand right beside Stella. Now Stella, put your hand on Toni's shoulder to give you support and help you balance while you move your right foot to the third post." Toni and Stella followed directions carefully. Stella made it successfully to the end of the wooden posts.

"Thank you, Toni, for collaborating," said Stella, smiling. She was so excited she clapped her hands, jumped up in the air, and twirled three times. On the ground, of course. Not on the wooden posts.

There were more activities, one with small rounded blocks that were close together and another with two long narrow pieces of wood that weren't so close together. At last they came to a long round pole a little over three inches or eight centimeters in diameter and raised slightly off the ground.

"Who wants to go first?" asked Guy the guide.

"Let me watch for a while," said Connor. "I want to observe before I try to walk the pole myself."

"Fair enough," said Guy the guide.

Aimi tried walking the pole like she'd walked the plank, one foot in front of the other. But Aimi lost her balance and stepped off the pole onto the ground.

Tad and Toni tried walking the pole, putting one foot in front of the other. Both lost their balance and had to step off the pole to keep from falling.

"I have an idea," said Connor. He stepped up onto the round pole, but instead of trying to put one foot in front of the other, Connor turned sideways. Arms outstretched, he moved sideways very slowly, sliding each foot a few inches at a time along the round pole. When he reached the end of the pole, everyone clapped and clapped.

"What did you learn?" asked Guy the guide.

"Sometimes it helps to watch before you actually try to do something new," said Toni.

"You may need a different strategy for something that looks very similar," said Aimi.

"Watching can be a coll-a-bor-ation strategy," said Stella. Everyone smiled. Guy the guide smiled, too, and high-fived Stella.

"Thank you, Grami," said the five LMC members, as they climbed into the car and buckled up for the ride home. "You are the best *Club* sponsor ever!"

"I'm glad you enjoyed that adventure," said Grami. "Did you have *fun* learning?"

"Oh, yes," said Connor.

"Me, too," said Tad and Toni at the same time.

"I learned a lot," said Stella. "Now I have to write down the metaphors I learned in *My Sleuth Notebook*."

"What's on your agenda for this afternoon, Connor?" asked Grami

"I'm doing what Stella is doing," said Connor. "I'm writing what I learned today in *My Sleuth Notebook*."

"I'm writing down my Daily Goals," said Aimi. "I definitely want to be healthy and balanced."

"Me, too," said Toni. "By the way, Grami, I had never heard of the Champion Challenge Course before today. How did you find out about it?"

"Your *Club* sponsor *sleuthed*," said Grami, "on her new computer."

"I'm for *sleuthing* about lunch," said Tad. "That's on my agenda, and I am starving, that's what. I trust our *Club* sponsor thought ahead about lunch?"

"Your *Club* sponsor did plan ahead," said Grami. "Lunch is waiting for us at home. Matter of fact, I'm hungry, too."

Then I'm going to write a verse about today's adventure," continued Tad." It was just great."

Stella yawned. "I think I'll take a wee nap after lunch. I bet Buddy-the-Beagle will take a wee nap with me."

"Ya *think*?" asked Connor, laughing.

"I *think*!" said Stella, also laughing.

And that's exactly what they did.

Nutrition can be like a huge mystery,
But you can solve it as you will see.
Choose healthful foods with variety,
In as natural a state as they can be.

6—Booting Up

"Grami," called Stella, "may I look something up on your computer?"

"Certainly," said Grami.

Stella went into the study and turned on the new computer. "Grami," she called, again, "what is a password? I want to *know*."

"Passwords are like a lock on the front door," said Grami, coming into the study. "You unlock the door when you want to enter the house. My new computer is like that. I boot it up and type in my password, which unlocks the computer. I'll enter the password for you."

"But at the Neo-Leo Wordpark I can use any computer without a password," said Stella, picturing the computers in her mind's eye. "Why? I want to *know*."

"Yes, you can. Those computers are for the general public," explained Grami. "No passwords are required. Personal computers are private and need a password."

"Could you give the members of the *Longevity Mystery Club* a password?" asked Stella. "And what does 'boot it up' mean? Your new computer has no boot. I want to *know*."

Grami smiled. "I'll call Jason and double check if we can create two passwords for this computer."

After Grami spoke with Jason, she said, "Stella, please tell the *LM Club* members to be here at eleven o'clock today. We'll create a *LM Club* password so you can access the computer. We'll also talk about 'booting it up.'"

At eleven o'clock, the five *LM Club* members—Tad and Toni, Aimi and Stella, and Connor—met in Grami's study. Their sponsor was in her favorite chair. Connor was curled up in his favorite beanbag. Tad was sitting on the hide-a-bed sofa, while Toni was cross-legged on the floor, her back against the sofa. Stella was sprawled on top of another beanbag beside their wee mascot, Buddy-the-Beagle, who was sound asleep on the rug.

"We need to create a *LM Club* password," said Grami. "It needs to have both capital and small letters and at least one number. I talked with Jason, and I know how to tell my computer to recognize two passwords: mine and yours."

"How about capital L and capital M and capital C?" suggested Toni.

"And the small letters could be *l-u-b*," said Aimi. "That spells the rest of the word Club."

"And there are five of us," said Tad. "Let's use the number five after the word Club."

"That's only six letters and one number," said Connor. "I think our password should be longer."

"I know!" cried Stella. "Let's use the word mascot!"

"We could spell *mascot* backwards, just to make the password more secure," suggested Aimi.

"What does our sponsor think?" asked Connor.

"Your *Club* sponsor thinks this is a strong password," said Grami. Everyone gathered around the new computer. Taking a small white card from the desk drawer,

Grami printed the password on it and pinned it to the cork bulletin board on the wall above the computer.

Stella was so excited she clapped her hands, jumped up in the air, and twirled three times. That wakened Buddy-the-Beagle, who stretched and yawned, looked around the room, decided there was nothing exciting to investigate and promptly went back to sleep.

"Now we need to memorize this password," said Tad. He looked carefully at the password Grami had written on the card, then closed his eyes and said aloud: "Capitols LMC, small *l-u-b*, the number 5, and small *t-o-c-s-a-m*. I've got it! LMClub5tocsam."

"Thank you for giving the *LM Club* members a club password to use on your computer," said Connor. "That's very generous, Grami. We appreciate it."

"What does jen-er-us mean?" asked Stella. "I want to *know*."

"It means that Grami did something for us that she didn't have to do," said Toni. "Like taking us on wonderful adventures."

"Oh," said Stella. "Yes, Grami. Thank you for being very jen-er-us."

"Do you want us to ask you each time we want to use the computer?" asked Aimi.

Grami shook her head. "That will not be necessary. I've watched each *LM Club* member use the computer properly and carefully."

"You always get first dibs," said Toni.

"First dibs?" asked Stella. "What is that? I want to *know*."

"Who can answer Stella's question?" asked Grami.

"I think it means a first claim on something," said Toni. "You have first dibs or first claim on the computer because you *own* it."

"I thought first dibs meant a *right* to something," said Tad.

"We could look it up on the computer," said Connor. "After all, we now have a password." That comment made everybody laugh.

"Let me look it up," cried Stella.

"Go ahead," said Grami, "although I am quite sure that both Toni and Tad are correct."

Stella read: "First dibs, a first claim to something to which no one else has a clearly recognized right." Everyone clapped.

"There will be plenty of time for everyone to use this computer," said Grami. "But thank you for recognizing first dibs."

"Grami," said Stella, "this morning you said we'd talk about 'booting up.' What is it? I want to *know*."

"Can anyone answer Stella's question?" asked Grami, looking at the other four *LM Club* members.

"I can," said Connor. "It means, Stella, that when Grami turns on her new computer, the software wakes up. Then, all she has to do is enter her password, and she can search the Internet or look in her files."

"I read about 'booting up your brain' at the Neo-Leo Wordpark," said Toni, opening her *My Sleuth Notebook*.

"Dr. Giuffre said that physical exercise helps the brain *boot up* efficiently, in much the same way as you would boot up a computer. I think it would be a crime to boot up your computer—but not your brain."

"Boot up the computer. Boot up my brain. What a hoot," said Stella, laughing.

"Boot. Hoot. I just thought of a riddle," said Tad. "What is alive and has four feet but owns no boot, although its name rhymes with boot?"

There was silence in the room, except for Buddy-the-Beagle's little snores. Finally Aimi said, "Let's list all the words we know that rhyme with boot. There's hoot and shoot and fruit and lute."

"And moot, flute, fruit, and chute," said Toni.

"I already said shoot," said Aimi. "S-h-o-o-t."

"But mine is spelled c-h-u-t-e," said Toni. "Like a parachute or laundry chute."

"Words are such fun," said Aimi, laughing.

"There's toot and root and uproot," said Connor. "I have an idea. Let's begin with the letter 'a' and go through the alphabet. Systematically. If our brains can't figure out this riddle, we can always ask Grami's new computer for help. After all, *we* have a password!"

"I'll write the words on our white board," said Grami, getting a special marker from the drawer. At the top she wrote and underlined boot: *b-o-o-t.* Beneath it she wrote absolute, beetroot, chute, coot, dilute, flute, fruit, hoot, root (r-o-o-t), route (r-o-u-t-e), and toot.

"There's jute," said Toni. "And kiwi fruit."

Grami kept writing.

"And loot and moot and mute," said Aimi, "but nothing for the letter 'n.'"

"Yes, there is!" cried Connor. "It's newt! N-e-w-t."

"You got it," said Tad.

"What's a newt?" asked Stella. "I want to *know*."

"A type of salamander," said Connor.

"I guess you'd know," said Toni, laughing. "You might become a veterinarian. A vet for creatures."

"While you were solving the riddle, I wrote a verse," said Tad. "How's this?"

"To solve a riddle we played a game,
Searching for a creature's name.
We tried out words that rhymed with boot,
And figured out its name was newt."

"Groovy!" shouted Stella. "I love that verse."

"Me too" said Grami. "You're quite the poet, Tad."

"Tad's a poet and doesn't know it!" said Toni, laughing. "I like the way your brain works, Tad." Everyone laughed at Toni's comment.

"Well, you *are* twins," said Connor. "I'd say you better like the way his brain works because yours is probably a lot like his!"

"But not identical," said Grami. "Even the brains of identical twins are not exactly the same because every thought you think changes your brain, and no two brains ever think identical thoughts. Besides, Tad and Toni are fraternal twins—just like any brother or sister, they just happened to grow and arrive on this planet together."

"Be sure to write these verses in your *My Sleuth Notebook*, Tad," said Aimi. "Someday you'll have a big collection. You might even publish a book!"

"That's exactly what I'm doing, Aimi," said Tad. "Grami, the five *LM Club* members have an idea for a very special adventure."

"Do tell," said Grami. "I like new ideas, especially if they represent a very special adventure."

Tad looked at Connor. Connor looked back at Tad and nodded. "A treehouse for our *LM Club*," said Connor. "In the big tree in your big back yard, Grami!"

"Connor's dad and our dad said they'd build it," said Tad. "That would be a very special adventure."

"If you agree, Grami, that is," said Toni.

"And Uncle Bob said he'd help," added Aimi.

"It would be great fun to have *Club* meetings in a treehouse," said Tad.

"With a basket for Buddy-the-Beagle," said Stella.

"And a small rocking chair for you, Grami," said Toni, "plus a cozy afghan and a little braided rug."

For her part, Grami was so surprised she sank right down on the stool beside the white board. But when she opened her mouth to say something, no sound came out.

"The neighbors have left-over boards from building their fence," said Aimi. "Maybe we could use those."

When Grami finally found her voice, she asked, "Did you say Uncle Bob thinks building a treehouse is a good idea?" The five *LM Club* members nodded.

"Uncle Bob even said he would help," said Aimi.

"You know," said Grami, thoughtfully. "I agree. A treehouse in the big tree in my big back yard would be absolutely doable and great fun for the *LM Club*."

"Hurray!" shouted Tad and Connor, high-fiving.

"Yay!" cried Aimi and Stella together.

"That would be so-o-o-o fabulous!" said Toni.

"On one condition," said Grami.

The *LM Club* members stopped talking and listened.

"If your dads and Uncle Bob will build the treehouse, I will pay for the supplies," said Grami. "The treehouse needs to be made of strong new wood so it will be sturdy and safe and last a long time."

"Our dads and Uncle Bob could come over Sunday morning and talk about drawing plans for the treehouse," said Connor, hopefully.

"Good idea," said Grami. "I'll fix Sunday brunch. We'll boot up our brains with good food and discuss the treehouse while we eat. Oh, my. This *is* exciting. When I was a little girl I wanted a tree house. Now I'll get it. "

The *LM Club* members jumped to their feet. Stella was so excited she clapped her hands, jumped up in the air, and twirled three times. And then she did it twice more for good measure. Aimi jumped up and down and up and down. Tad and Connor danced a jig all around the room while Toni did some jazzercise moves. Naturally all the clapping and jumping and jigging and jazzercising waked Buddy-the-Beagle, who promptly threw back his head, pointed his little nose in the air, opened his little mouth, and began to howl his *I'm-so-happy* howl. Grami did not clap or jump or dance a jig. She just moved from the stool to sit in her favorite chair.

"Grami," said Aimi, when all the jumping and jigging and dancing and howling had stopped, "you look a little dazed. You know, surprised." She added that for Stella's benefit.

"I think I am a little stunned," said Grami, "but in a good way. It's a wonderful idea. When exactly did you detectives think of this very special adventure, as you put it?"

"Last weekend," said Connor. "Dad and I were watching a TV program about people who build treehouses when the twins' father stopped by. I said 'Sure would be fun to have a *LM Club* treehouse.' He and my dad looked at each other and said, 'Well, why not?'"

"When our dad came home, he told us about the idea," said Toni, picking up the story. "Then he called your brother, Uncle Bob, who said he'd help our dads build a treehouse for the *LM Club*—if you agreed."

"Did you know about this?" Grami asked Stella and Aimi. Both girls nodded, smiling.

Aimi said, "Toni called our candy red mobile last night, but we decided not to say anything until we could all ask you today, together."

"And you agreed, right?" asked Connor. He wanted to be very sure.

I certainly did," said Grami, laughing. "It's absolutely phantasmagorical, and I just made up that word, Stella, so no point in asking me about it. I wish I'd thought of a treehouse myself. After all, I am the *Club* sponsor."

"But you told us that no one person can think of everything," piped up Stella.

Grami nodded. "I did. It reminds me of that old saying that no one is an island. We need each other."

"We *have* each other," said Aimi. "We are *LM Club* members and you're our sponsor."

"And Buddy-the-Beagle is our mascot," said Stella. "Remember our mascot!"

"A very special adventure," mused Tad. His comment triggered a great deal of laughter that soon turned into a serious discussion about the new treehouse.

"We could have a ladder up to the treehouse," said Stella. "Grami, can you climb a ladder?"

"We could have stairs instead of a ladder," said Tad, quickly, "if that would be easier for you."

"And you *are* getting slimmer," said Aimi, kindly.

"We'll see what your dads and Uncle Bob have to say on Sunday," said Grami.

"Let's go to the Neo-Leo Wordpark this afternoon," said Toni, "so we can all look up building supplies at the same time."

"Good idea," said Grami.

"While there, maybe we can research possible treehouse designs, too," said Tad.

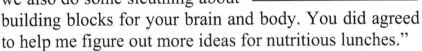

"Speaking of building supplies," said Grami, "I suggest we also do some sleuthing about building blocks for your brain and body. You did agreed to help me figure out more ideas for nutritious lunches."

"My teacher says garbage in, garbage out," said Toni. "I want to avoid putting garbage in my body. That's a good idea for research, Grami."

"Definitely," said Grami. "And that's one reason I offered to spring for the building materials." Stella opened her mouth, so Grami quickly added, "Purchase them. I want to be certain we get high quality building materials for a safe treehouse."

"Can we eat first?" asked Tad. "I'm sure I could do better detective work after a good lunch."

Grami laughed. "Come into the kitchen, and we'll fix lunch together. Everyone can help."

They ate home-made sandwiches, this time on rye sourdough instead of white bread. There were fresh apples and bananas, carrot sticks, and dry roasted nuts. They munched away until even Tad said he was full.

"Next time you're checking the oil in your car, Grami, I'll bring you a carrot so you can have a healthy energy snack," said Stella.

"Where in the world did that idea come from?" asked Grami.

"I don't know," said Stella, laughing. "I just thought  of it while I was eating a carrot stick."

After lunch the five sleuths and their sponsor got into Grami's car. "Do you each have your *My Sleuth Notebook* and pen?" asked Grami.

"I do," said five voices in unison. At that, Grami started the car and drove to the Neo-Leo Wordpark.

"We have two hours for research," said Grami. "Select your computer and let's get cracking."

"Get busy," said Aimi before Stella could ask what 'cracking' meant.

"I'm ready to sleuth on a computer by myself," said Stella. "I'll ask for help if I get stuck."

"That's fine with me," said Grami, sitting down at a computer across from Stella. "I have a long list of things to look up."

"I'll spend half the time researching building supplies for our *Club* treehouse," said Connor, "and then research building supplies for my *BrainBody House*. I like that name."

"So do I," said Grami. "That's exactly what it is."

They had been at the Neo-Leo Wordpark for almost an hour when Tad came over to speak to Grami. "The librarian says they're showing a special IMAX film about the human body. May we watch it?"

"How long is the film?" asked Grami in a soft voice, but not whispering. "When does it begin?"

"It starts in 10 minutes and lasts about 45 minutes," said Tad.

Grami looked at her watch. "We can do that," she said. "Round up the *LM Club* members, and we'll get in line. I'd like to see that myself."

An hour later, as they left the IMAX Theater, Aimi exclaimed, "That was amazing! Simply amazing!"

"Let's debrief," said Tad, as they drove home.

"Good idea," said Grami. "Tell me something new you learned from watching the IMAX film."

"I learned that the largest cell in a human body is the female egg, the only cell visible to the naked eye," said Tad. "The smallest cell is the male sperm."

"But it's powerful!" said Connor, chuckling.

"I learned that stomach acid is strong enough to dissolve razor blades," said Aimi. "Yikes."

"The average person will produce enough saliva during a lifetime to fill two swimming pools," said Connor. "But I don't know how big the pools would be."

"In thirty minutes your body gives off enough heat to bring two quarts of water to a boil," said Tad.

"Teeth are the only part of the human body that are unable to repair themselves," said Toni.

"It takes forty-three muscles to frown and only seventeen to smile," said Stella. "Who would want to spend the extra energy to frown? I want to *know*."

"Good question," said Connor, "but I guess you'd have to ask someone who is frowning."

"Shall we meet tomorrow morning and share what we learned about building materials for the treehouse?" asked Grami as she turned into her driveway. "We can talk about quality building blocks for the human body, too: our *BrainBody House*."

The five *LM Club* members agreed to meet at ten o'clock the next morning.

At ten the following morning the *LM Club* members and their sponsor gathered in Grami's study. "Who wants to begin debriefing?" she asked.

"Just think!" cried Stella, excitedly. "Soon we can meet in our own *LM Club* treehouse!"

"I learned that bamboo is light and strong," said Tad. "It might make a good floor."

"I saw a picture of a bamboo bed that could be for Buddy-the-Beagle, our wee mascot," said Stella.

"Well, it wouldn't fit any of us," said Tad.

"Are you teasing me, Tad?" asked Stella. "Again?"

"Of course he is," said Toni. "Tad only teases people he likes. Most boys *only* tease people they like."

"I asked *Tad*," said Stella seriously.

"Toni's right," said Tad. "Boys only tease people they like. I like you and your sense of humor."

"Plus, you're thinking light-weight things for the *LM Club* treehouse, Stella," said Aimi. "That's a good idea."

Stella smiled. She was so pleased she clapped her hands, jumped up in the air, and twirled three times.

Grami smiled, too. "What did you sleuths learn about building blocks for your *BrainBody House*? I learned that that the brain needs fuel right away in the morning and according to Dr. Andrew Weil, healthier carbs are the best source for brain cells."

"I read," said Toni, "that eating breakfast helps boost brain function. Students who ate breakfast had 40 percent higher math grades, were half as likely to be sad, and were less hyperactive. That's a lot of benefits."

"I read that sourdough bread with only wild yeast sourdough starter is a better choice than either commercial white or brown bread," said Tad. "The wheat is partially digested."

"I learned that sugar, white flour, white rice, and refined and processed foods made with them are poor-quality building blocks," said Aimi.

"So are fried foods like potato chips and French fries," said Stella. "But fresh fruits and vegetables are good-quality building blocks. That's what I learned."

"I know!" cried Aimi. "After the planning meeting, on Sunday, let's go through the pantry and remove any foods that are poor-quality building blocks."

"Good idea," said Grami. "From now on I'm buying only quality foods for *Longevity Mystery Club* members—and their sponsor."

Sunday morning dawned bright and beautiful. No surprise, Grami's brunch was a smash hit.

"Well, we sure polished that off," said Uncle Bob, patting his stomach and smiling contentedly. "It was splendiferous!"

"What did we polish off and what was splen-dif-er-ous?" asked Stella. "I want to *know*."

"Brunch," said Uncle Bob, laughing. "Now, let's get this tree-house planning meeting under way."

A great deal of talking and walking around the big tree in Grami's back yard followed as they took measurements here, there, and everywhere—even up in the big tree—while Uncle Bob made notes on his iPad. Finally Uncle Bob closed his iPad, stretched, and said: "We've got this nailed. We'll go and start drawing plans and leave you all to dream about your *Longevity Mystery Club* Treehouse."

And that's exactly what they did.

I'm glad to know there are four PIs,
That live in my brain behind my eyes.
Each one assists me day after day,
To help me be wiser in every way.

7—Hidden Treasure

"Grami," said Aimi, excitedly, "my music teacher is helping me with the *Longevity Mystery Club* song."

"I knew she would," said Grami.

"I like the tune," said Toni. "It's turning out to be a really good song." Pausing for a moment, she added, "Guess what? I'm really hungry."

"You're what?" asked Aimi, in surprise.

"I'm hungry," Toni repeated, a puzzled note in her voice. Everyone looked at her in amazement.

"Tad's the one who's always hungry!" said Stella.

"When did you eat last, Toni?" asked Aimi.

"Oh, a couple hours ago," she replied.

"Is your body out of energy?" asked Grami. "Does it need food to give you energy?"

"I don't know," said Toni. "But if my body doesn't need energy, how come I'm hungry?"

"It could be a tapeworm," said Connor. "I just read about tapeworms on the Internet."

"Really, Connor. It's highly unlikely Toni has a tapeworm," said Tad. "Stop scaring the girl."

"Are you thirsty?" asked Grami. "Sometimes it is hard to tell the difference between hunger and thirst. Try drinking a glass of water. If you are thirsty, your hunger pangs tend to disappear in a few minutes."

"And if I'm not hungry *or* thirsty?" asked Toni.

"Then perhaps your brain is upset about something," said Grami.

"Maybe that's it," said Toni, slowly.

"Your brain may be trying to get you do to something to help you feel better," said Grami. "When food is involved, it's called emotional eating."

Toni looked at the floor, then out the window. Finally she said, "Well, I just learned that a friend of mine is moving away. I'm sad she is going to live in another town. I'll really miss her at school."

"That's too bad," said Aimi. "I'd be sad, too."

"So," said Grami, thoughtfully, "a PI in your brain is trying to help you understand that your friend moving away is a loss for you, and your PI wants you to do something to help yourself feel better."

"What's a PI?" asked Stella. "I want to *know*."

"A PI is a *Private Investigator*," said Tad.

"And you have four PI's that go everywhere with you, paying attention to what is going on in the environment, inside and outside of you," Grami continued. "They are joy, anger, fear, and sadness."

"That's amazing," said Connor. "And here I was thinking that ..."

"Does Buddy-the-Beagle have four PI's living in his brain, too?" asked Stella, interrupting. "I want to *know*."

"Stella, you interrupted Connor," said Grami. "When someone is talking, please wait 'til they're done."

"Sorry, Connor," said Stella, looking at the floor.

"No worries," said Connor, "and that is actually a very interesting question. What do you think, Grami?"

"You are the five *LM Club* sleuths," replied Grami. "What do you think?"

"I think Buddy-the-Beagle does have the four PI's," said Aimi, in her soft sweet voice. "He sings his very sad *I'm-sorry-for-myself* howl when he has to stay home and his *I-want-to-be-with-you* howl when he is lonesome."

"I believe you are correct," said Grami.

"And Buddy-the-Beagle has his *I'm-happy* howl," said Toni. "The day he became our *LM Club* mascot he sat in the middle of the room and howled his *I'm happy* howl."

"And we all laughed and laughed," said Tad.

"Remember that big storm when Buddy-the-Beagle was afraid?" asked Connor. "That's when I heard his *I'm-so-scared* howl."

"He actually hid under Grami's bed," said Stella. "I had to crawl under, too, and keep him company for a long time before he was willing to come out."

"When Buddy-the-Beagle is mad, he doesn't howl," said Tad. "He growls. He doesn't growl often, but when he does he sounds *really* mad. Remember when our neighbors brought their new puppy over and it started to eat Buddy-the-Beagle's dinner? Buddy definitely growled his *I'm-angry* growl."

"So, I have four PI's that give me clues," said Connor, holding up four fingers. "Joy. Anger. Fear. Sadness."

"Right you are," said Grami, nodding. "Those four

PI's—joy, anger, fear, and sadness—provide tips they think you need to know. Most likely Buddy-the-Beagle has his own doggie PI's as well, Stella."

"Let's go to the Neo-Leo Wordpark today," said Tad. "I really want to investigate those four PI's."

"We can do that," said Grami. "The *LM Club* members are becoming excellent detectives."

"It's so much fun," said Toni. "It's like searching for hidden treasure!"

"And knowledge may be the ultimate treasure," said Grami. "Hidden—*until* you search and discover it."

"I didn't even know how long I wanted to live until we learned about those very very *very* old supercentenarians," said Stella. "I like searching for hidden treasure! I like being alive, too." She was so excited she clapped her hands, jumped up in the air, and twirled three times, as she usually did when she was very very happy.

"I'm ready to sleuth at the Neo-Leo Wordpark," said Tad.

"Then let's do it," said Grami. The five sleuths got into her car and fastened their seatbelts.

"How much time do we have today?" asked Toni.

"Two hours," said Grami, pulling into the car park and shutting off the engine. "Two whole hours."

"*Car park?*" asked Stella, pointing to a sign. "What's that? I want to *know*!"

"It's just another name for a parking lot," said Aimi.

Two hours later, as they were driving away from the Neo-Leo Wordpark, Connor said, "Those two hours went by very fast. I wish we had a computer at my house. Then I could be an Internet sleuth any time I need to look up something. I'll ask my dad if we can buy one."

"That's a good idea," said Grami. "I'm certainly enjoying sleuthing on my new computer. I learned some very interesting things about my brain today."

"After we eat," said Tad, "can we debrief? I'd like to know what you learned about the brain, Grami."

Back at Grami's, the five *LM Club* members and their sponsor sat down to a delicious lunch. After they had eaten and cleaned up the kitchen, they all went into the study. "Okay," said Grami, "let's debrief."

"I added PI to my list of synonyms for detectives," said Stella, quickly. "PI, for Private Investigator."

"I learned lots and lots," said Connor. "But I couldn't find out exactly where my four PI's live."

"Fortunately, that's part of what I learned today," said Grami. "Make fists with your hands and put them together, thumbs touching." The five detectives did what Grami asked. "Now, pretend that you have a gray glove on your left hand and a white glove on your right hand."

"Gloves," said Connor. "Are they made of leather? Leather gloves are cool."

"Not if the weather is hot," said Tad, laughing.

"I'm not talking temperature!" said Connor, rolling his eyes. "I'm talking, *cool.* You know, smart looking."

"I know," said Tad. "Just joking."

Aimi looked at her hands, imagining a gray glove on the left fist and a white glove on the right.

"How come the right glove is a lighter color than the left?" asked Aimi.

Grami explained. "The right side of the brain contains more axons, that long projection from a neuron that is wrapped with myelin, a whitish-colored insulation. Think fiber optics. Although emotions impact every cell in your body, imagine that your PI's have headquarters in one of your two brain hemispheres. Who researched joy?"

"I did," said Toni, opening her *My Sleuth Notebook.* "The joy PI tells you that everything is going well in life. It's the only PI that has no negative outcomes when you maintain it over time. Joy helps you en*joy* being alive."

"Brain scans, computer pictures taken while a brain is alive," said Grami, "have shown that when an individual is joyful, the left hemisphere lights up."

"The gray glove represents my left hemisphere," said Tad, looking at his left hand.

"Right," said Grami.

"Uh-h. I thought you said a gray glove was on my left hand," said Tad.

"I did," said Grami. "That's exactly what I said."

"But you just said *right*," said Tad.

"I meant the *right* that means *correct*," said Grami.

"Oh, that's funny!" said Aimi, laughing. "Words, words, words. Right and *right*. I like words."

Grami laughed, too, and then continued talking.

"Brain scans have also shown that when people are angry, fearful, or sad, their brain's right hemisphere lights up. Those three PI's are sometimes called "protective" emotions because they give you information to help you stay safe and protect—or take care of yourself.""

"The white glove represents my brain's *right* hemisphere," said Tad. "Three protective PI's hang out and have their headquarters in my right hemisphere. Correct?"

"Metaphorically correct," said Grami, laughing. "Now, who researched anger?"

"I did," said Connor, opening his *My Sleuth Notebook*. He read: "Anger tells you that your personal boundaries have been invaded and it gives you energy to set appropriate personal limits. If you can't recognize anger and manage it correctly, you may allow others to take advantage of you or even begin to tolerate the intolerable. Unmanaged anger, however, can lead to bitterness, illness, ulcers, and even death."

"I heard about a driver who cut in front of another car on the highway," said Aimi. "The second driver became angry, sped up, and rammed the first driver's car. The cars exploded and both drivers died."

"Your anger PI alerts you when someone invades your personal boundaries or personal space," said Grami. "It gives you energy to take *appropriate* action."

"Like calling the police if a driver is acting crazy and might be drunk," said Toni, "rather than staying angry, ramming the other car, and creating a bad accident."

"Or a student cuts ahead of you in line at school," said Tad. "That's invading your space boundaries."

"It was his problem," said Connor. "We just moved to another spot because we didn't want a fight." Grami nodded.

"I saw a girl say something unkind to another student and that student just walked the other way," said Aimi. Grami nodded again.

"I chose to play with a different boy at school because the one I was playing with kept breaking the rules," said Connor. Grami nodded a third time.

"Or forgiving the neighbor's dog when it digs up your flowers," said Stella.

"And forgiving the person who *owns* the dog," said Grami, chuckling. "Yes, all of the above are examples of taking appropriate actions. Your EQ, or Emotional Intelligence, helps you choose appropriate behaviors."

"EQ, EQ, EQ!" cried Stella.

"If your EQ is low," Grami went on, "you may misuse the information your anger PI gives you or use the energy inappropriately. For example, beating up on the student who cut into line or yelling at the one who said something unkind or being rude to the student who broke the rules or running into the car that cut you off—when you have your own car and a driver's license."

"And risk wrecking my own car?" asked Connor. "Not likely. I'll use my PI's to be wise, not stupid."

"Retaliating is an unwise use of the energy your anger PI gives you," said Grami. "Retaliation can hurt others, but it can certainly hurt you, too."

"Yeah," said Aimi, "Like the drivers who got mad at each other. They both died! That was really dumb." The others nodded.

"What is re-tal-i-a-shun?" asked Stella. "I want to *know*."

"It means doing something unkind to the person who hurt you or treated you badly in order to get revenge," said Grami. "Tit-for-tat is rarely a good idea."

"Re-tal-i-a-shun is low EQ," said Stella.

"You got it, Stella," said Grami. "And you want high levels of EQ."

"I looked up *fear*," said Tad, "because I remembered how scared Joel was at the Riddle-Bee. Your fear PI lets you know that you're in some type of danger— unless it's an imaginary fear and you're really in no actual danger at all. It gives you energy to take appropriate action to protect yourself and others. If you don't manage your fear, it can kill ideas, undermine confidence, and turn into phobias or immobilization," said Tad, reading from his *My Sleuth Notebook*. "When Joel started using helpful self-talk, he stopped being scared. That helped him win!"

"Your experience with Joel is an example of how an imaginary fear can negatively impact you," agreed Grami. "It can definitely interfere with what you are trying to do and sabotage your success. "Your fear PI not only alerts you to danger and helps you pay attention but also gives you energy to step away or run and hide or find help, if necessary," said Grami. "Unless it is imagined fear. Then, you can expend a lot of worry and anxiety energy for nothing."

"I once heard a girl say she was 'sick with fear,'" said Aimi. "I guess it's real. After all, Joel was sick."

"He was sick because he was scared of forgetting and didn't know how to talk to his brain," said Tad. "But in Joel's case there wasn't really any danger."

Grami nodded and smiled at Toni. "Since your sad PI got your attention earlier today, I'm guessing you sleuthed sadness and loss. Am I correct?"

"You guessed right, Grami," said Toni.

"You guessed *correctly*," said Tad, laughing.

Toni smiled at her twin brother and opened her *My Sleuth Notebook*. "Sadness helps you recognize that you have experienced a loss in your life and it gives you energy to grieve successfully and move on," she read. "Without sadness you might not recover from your losses, get stuck in sadness, and  feel bad all the time." Toni turned the page and continued. "If you stay stuck in sadness you may get sick, suppress your immune system, and decrease your levels of ser ... sero ..."

"Serotonin," said Grami. "It's a brain chemical."

"Of serotonin in your brain and GI tract," said Toni.

"Your GI or gastrointestinal tract is your stomach and intestines," said Aimi, before Stella could even open her mouth to ask the question.

"And you might even get depressed—really *really* sad—and just sit around and do nothing," continued Toni, closing her notebook.

"Since you often feel better after eating, your sadness PI probably prompted you to feel hungry, Toni," said Grami. "EQ can help you assess what your PI is trying to tell you and assist you in making a good decision about a course of action, what to do."

"You were right," said Toni. "My body didn't need food. I was sad because my classmate is moving away."

"Grami was *correct*," said Connor.

"Yes," said Toni, laughing. "She was correct. My sadness PI gave me energy to grieve that loss, and my EQ helped me figure out a plan."

"What plan?" asked Stella. "I want to *know*."

"A plan to stay in touch with each other," said Toni. "During the two years her father has to work in that town, we can text, email, Skype, tweet, do Facetime, or talk by phone. We can even write a letter on the computer, print it off, put a stamp on the envelope, and post it for delivery. With a plan, I feel less sad—and I not so hungry."

"Bravo," said Grami, smiling.

"I think that's good detective work," said Tad.

"I think it's excellent sleuthing," said Connor.

"And high EQ, too," said Stella.

"Yes, it's all those," agreed Grami. "Toni's sadness PI helped her identify and grieve the loss and EQ helped her select an appropriate behavior and make a plan."

"I like this PI business," said Connor. "Four Private Investigators, and I don't even have to pay their salaries."

"I'm glad you're getting to know your four PI's," said Grami. "They stay alert to what is going on around you and inside you. And they give you information and energy when they sense it could be helpful."

"How do they get our attention?" asked Aimi.

"Typically by changing something in your brain and body," said Grami. "For example, your heart may beat faster or you may breathe shallowly or even hold your breath. Your face might flush or the palms of your hands could get sweaty or you might need to use the toilet. You could feel hungry or nauseated or feel like butterflies are in your stomach. You might suddenly feel distracted or forget things you usually remember."

"You might even throw up, like Joel did," said Tad.

"Or feel sad and then hungry, like I did," said Toni.

"When you notice changes in your body," said Grami, "ask yourself this: Is one of my PI's trying to get my attention so it can give me clues and information?"

"It's a little like magic," said Aimi. "When Tad taught Joel about the white bear phenomenon, he stopped being scared."

"What Tad told him," Grami explained, "helped Joel realize there was no real danger. That gave him the opportunity to make a different choice, especially when Tad helped him learn how to change his self-talk. It's not really magic and yet, in a way, it is. What you tell your brain is very powerful."

"We've been using EQ all summer to practice our musical instruments before we go on an adventure," said Stella. "Tell me more about EQ. I want to *know*."

"EQ helps you use the information your PI's give you to make good choices. Think of it as using your heart and your head in balance," said Grami. "When you delay starting on your adventure until your practicing is done, you are 'delaying gratification' for a bigger long-term reward."

"That's because taking music lessons and practicing builds software in our brain," said Tad. "My teacher told us about that at school."

Grami nodded. "People with low levels of EQ skills often get themselves in trouble by choosing unhelpful behaviors, three of which are called JOT behaviors."

"What is a JOT behavior?" asked Stella. "J-O-T. I want to *know*."

"*LM Club* is an acronym, a short way to say the *Longevity Mystery Club*," Grami explained. "JOT is an acronym that stands for three unhelpful behaviors that represent low levels of EQ. The *J* stands for jumping to conclusions, *O* is for overreacting, and *T* is for taking things personally."

"Oh, oh," said Aimi. "I see how that works. The driver who got cut off may have jumped to the conclusion that the first driver cut him off just to be mean. He might have been angry about something, but he might have had a heart attack or gotten distracted. There could have been several reasons for his cutting off the second driver."

"Then the second driver overreacted," said Toni.

"And took it personally," said Tad, picking up the conversation. "He chose to ram the first driver's car."

"But because of JOT behaviors," said Connor, "both drivers died. That was a big waste. And expensive, besides. Two funerals. And think of their families and how sad they might be because two family members were killed. Maybe a father or son or brother or cousin…"

"I guess that's what you meant, Grami, when you said that retaliation can hurt others but it can hurt yourself, too," said Tad, slowly.

Ri . . ." Grami started to say. And then she stopped and said instead, "Correct, Tad."

"This is such fun!" cried Stella. "EQ and JOT. JOT and EQ. We're detectives, *and* we're learning word shorthand—ack-ron-ims." She was so excited she clapped her hands, jumped up in the air, and twirled three times.

"My teacher talked about deferring rewards," said Connor. "That's the same thing as delayed gratification, right? I mean *correct*?" he added, laughing.

"You are correct, Connor," said Grami. "Both terms refer to the skill or ability of waiting patiently for a bigger reward that isn't here yet. It is one of the key skills related to high levels of Emotional Intelligence."

"High, high EQ," said Stella. "I want high, high, *HIGH* EQ!"

"You are such a jumping jack," said Aimi, laughing.

"Some brains learn best—if they learn at all—when the bodies that carry them around are moving," said Grami. "My brain's opinion is that Stella may have that type of brain. It needs to move around to learn easily."

At that, Stella clapped her hands, jumped up in the air, and twirled three times—singing, "I'm learning and moving! I'm moving and learning!" over and over again.

"Are my four PI's all girls?" asked Aimi. "Because I'm a girl, you know."

"We know, we *know*," said Tad, laughing.

"Do we *ever* know!" said Connor, also laughing.

"But that is a good question," said Tad. "Are my four PI's all boys? And no comments from the peanut gallery because Connor and I *know* we're boys." They high-fived each other.

"Think of them any way that makes sense to you," said Grami. "I think of mine as neither boys nor girls. Just PI's. This afternoon you might want to draw pictures of what each of your four PIs look like. They'll all look slightly different because each of your brains is different."

Tad and Connor looked at each other. "We can have fun with this," said Connor. Tad nodded.

"I like knowing I have four PI's," said Stella, clapping her hands. "How come you didn't tell us sooner, Grami? I want to *know*."

"Really, Stella," said Aimi, patiently. "If Grami told us everything all at once we wouldn't remember it all, so she tells us a little bit at a time."

"I'm hungry," said Tad, "and it's not because I'm mad or scared or sad or even happy. My body just needs food for energy. I can tell the difference."

"Well, it *is* time for lunch," said Grami, laughing. "And I'm pleased you are learning to know when your body needs food. Come along, everyone. Eat up."

"After lunch I'm drawing pictures of my four PI's. My *own* Private Investigators," said Connor. "I can hardly wait to see what they look like!"

The other *LM Club* members nodded in agreement.

And that's exactly what they did.

Preventive plans you must maintain,
If healthy brains you would retain.
Safety first is quite germane—
For both your body and your brain.

8—Safety Sabotage

"Oh, Grami!" whispered Aimi, looking out of the kitchen window. "The two dads and Uncle Bob have started building the *Longevity Mystery Club* treehouse. It looks like part of the floor is done!"

"So it is," said Grami, moving to stand beside Aimi. "They will likely make even more progress today while we're away on our next adventure."

"Buddy-the-Beagle will watch," said Stella.

"Please put the *LM Club* mascot in the screened-in porch," said Grami. "That will keep him out of harm's way, and no one will have to look out for him. Make sure his water dish is full, and he has dried dog food. We may not return from our adventure until late this evening."

The doorbell rang twice. "That'll be Tad and Toni and Connor, right on time. Ten o'clock sharp," said Aimi. "Guess what?" she asked as she opened the front door. "I've almost finished writing the *LM Club* song."

"Yay!" cried Tad, Toni, and Connor all together.

"May I help you carry water and our healthier lunch to the car?" Tad asked Grami as he walked into the kitchen.

"Thank you, Tad," said Grami. "You may put water in the trunk, because water is important for the brain and the body. But no lunch. Part of today's adventure involves eating lunch in a new restaurant."

"Hmm-m," said Tad, eyes wide. "Food. That should be fun."

"Okay!" cried Stella, barreling into the room. "Buddy-the-Beagle is all good."

"Inventory time," said Grami. "Walking shoes, 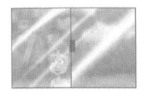 jackets, sunglasses, and *My Sleuth Notebooks*?" Five hands waved enthusiastically. "Then into the car we go. Buckle up. Our first stop is at the Neo-Leo Wordpark. That's part one of this adventure."

"How come you want us to bring sunglasses?" asked Stella. "I want to *know*."

"My eye doctor says that wearing sunglasses when you're out in the bright sun helps protect your retina, that movie screen at the back of each eyeball. It may help prevent the development of something called macular degeneration, which can impair your vision."

"Oh," said Stella. "Good to know. I want to still see clearly when I reach the age of 122 years and 164 days, just like that very very *very* old French lady!"

"What would you like us to research this morning, Grami?" asked Toni.

"Your mission," replied Grami, "is to identify a couple of things you can do to protect your brain, to keep it safe, and to prevent injury. We have thirty minutes for part one of today's adventure."

"That should be easy and fun," said Connor.

"And part two of today's adventure is eating lunch in a new restaurant, *right*?" asked Tad.

"*Correct,*" said Grami, and everyone laughed.

"And part three?" asked Stella. "I want to *know*!"

"Stella, you know *LM Club* adventures are usually a secret surprise. Grami never answers that question until she is ready to tell us," said Aimi, in her soft sweet voice.

"I know, I know," said Stella, smiling. "But I thought Grami might tell us this time. Let's see. We have walking shoes, jackets, sunglasses, and notebooks. That does not tell us anything specific."

"Sure doesn't," said Toni, giggling. "We take those with us on almost every adventure."

"Here we are at the Neo-Leo Wordpark," said Grami, pulling into a parking space. "Let's get to it. We'll debrief on the drive to the new restaurant."

Before long, five *LM Club* members and their sponsor were heads down, each at a computer in the Librivox Zone of the 21st century library. The five detectives actually were surprised when Grami said it was time to go.

"That thirty minutes went by like *greased lightning*," exclaimed Tad, closing his *Notebook*.

Soon they were back in Grami's car and out on the highway heading toward part two of the adventure.

"What did you learn about brain safety?" asked Grami. "About things that could sabotage your brain?"

"What does that word mean?" asked Stella. "I want to *know*."

"*Sabotage* means things that might hurt, damage, or destroy something," said Grami, "like your brain cells."

"Which one of us would you like to start the debriefing, Grami?" asked Toni.

"We often begin with Aimi," said Grami, with a twinkle in her eye. "This time let's debrief in reverse alphabetical order by first names. So, who goes first?"

"Me," said Toni, opening her *My Sleuth Notebook.* "Avoid smoking or breathing in side-smoke from tobacco products that others are using, because tobacco smoke takes up space in the air that would have been used for oxygen. I'm sure glad there are smoke-free restaurants!"

"I'm next," said Tad. "Exercise away from busy highways to avoid breathing in vehicle exhaust—for the same reason. Exhaust takes up space in the air that needs to be used for oxygen. And avoid poisons and pesticides."

"Excellent, Toni and Tad," said Grami.

"We need to put away those two little throw rugs," said Stella. "Tripping on rugs can cause falls that could hurt your head. I always wear a seatbelt to avoid hitting my head if an accident happens."

"Plus, it keeps you from jumping up in the air and twirling when you're in the car," said Connor, laughing.

"I'm glad you're a good driver, Grami," said Aimi. "And you watch out for other drivers, too."

"Thank you," said Grami. "Let me think. We could put one little throw rug in Buddy-the-Beagle's basket in the new *LM Club* treehouse."

"And put the other one under your rocking chair," said Connor. "My turn." Opening his *Notebook* he read, "Wear a helmet when you skateboard or play sports like soccer or rugby or football or hockey, or if you are boxing, and whenever you ride a bike." He paused for a moment. "Do you think that very very *very* old French lady—as Stella puts it—wore a helmet when she rode her bike until she was 100? Head trauma can result in dementia. That's very scary! I sure wouldn't want to lose *my* memory!"

"And what is da-men-cha?" asked Stella. "Is it a cha-cha for men? I want to *know*."

"It's when your brain doesn't work right because it has been injured or damaged," said Toni.

"That's right *and* correct," said Grami. "People with dementia often forget things, have difficulty paying attention, and may become irritable and depressed or even apathetic." And before Stella could ask a question, Grami quickly added, "*Apathetic* means they don't seem to be interested in or care about much of anything."

"I was just going to ask what a-path-e-tic meant," said Stella, laughing. "Now I don't need to ask. I *know!*"

Aimi opened her *My Sleuth Notebook*. "Whenever possible, protect your brain by avoiding contact with infectious organisms because some diseases can attack the brain and cause problems. Like Meningitis. Even flu or a cold can turn into something serious."

"Along that same line," said Grami, "I read an article that suggested it's a good idea to text or email or phone friends who are sick instead of visiting them in person and getting exposed to their germs. It's easy to do that with my mobile phone and with email on my new computer. Plus, the author said that sometimes visiting in person can be tiring for someone who is sick."

They drove along in silence for a while, watching the interesting scenery fly by.

"Hey, look at that huge sign," said Connor, looking out of the car window. *"Exploratorium Town.* Now that looks interesting."

"I'm glad you think so," said Grami. "It's our destination. Think of an Exploratorium as a place where visitors have the opportunity for some hands-on experiences."

"Part two of today's adventure is lunch," said Tad. "I am so-o-o-o ready for *that* hands-on experience."

"And here is the new restaurant," said Grami, parking the car. *"Mum's Munchies."*

"What a great name," said Aimi.

"The words *Mum's Munchies* both start with the letter 'm' and that's called alliteration," said Toni. "We just learned about that in school."

Grami smiled. "That's correct, Toni. And while we eat lunch, you'll get to learn about part three of today's adventure."

Inside *Mum's Munchies*, a waitress showed them to their table and gave each a menu. When she returned to take their orders, she had six large cards in her hand.

"What are those about?" asked Connor.

"These cards list the activities that are offered here at *Exploratorium Town,"* said the waitress. "Let me take your orders and then you can start reviewing the options and making your choices."

"Each of you may select one activity," said Grami. "This is an opportunity for your brain to have a hands-on experience with something you have never done before."

The five *LM Club* members and their sponsor read  the list of activities while they ate. "We each get a personal coach!" exclaimed Aimi. "That is so-o-o cool!"

"Oh, look," cried Connor. "Fencing is on the list. I choose fencing. Want to come with me, Tad?"

Tad shook his head. "Thanks but no thanks. I want to climb that rock wall. Hope it's a high one."

"What are you choosing, Grami?" asked Aimi.

"Turtle Turf," said Grami, pointing to a picture on the brochure. "They have many kinds of turtles here, including some giant land tortoises that can live well over 100 years. I want to meet, greet, and feed those centenarians—up close and personal."

"I've decided on indoor skydiving," said Toni. "It looks fun and exciting in the picture."

"Archery is my choice," said Aimi. "I want to shoot real arrows with a real bow."

"I choose indoor skydiving, *and* shooting arrows with a real bow, *and* jumping on the giant bungee trampoline," said Stella, excitedly.

"You need to choose one activity," said Grami.

"But I want to do *three*," said Stella. "I can't choose just one when I like all three."

"Today we each choose one activity only," said Grami. "Perhaps we can return another time and try a different one. You and your brain can choose one today."

"But I want to do three!" Stella repeated, a tear rolling down her cheek. "My brain can't choose only one, because I want to do three."

"Can't choose only one activity, Stella, or won't?" asked Aimi. "Your brain can choose only one, you know."

Stella shook her head and brushed a tear away.

"Help your brain choose," said Grami.

"How?" asked Stella. "How can I help my brain choose only one activity? I want to *know*!"

"You help it choose by giving it only two options at a time," Grami said patiently, "because your brain only has two hemispheres. Ask yourself: 'Stella, would you prefer archery or the giant bungee trampoline?' Take a minute and think about it."

"Oh, more of this choosing business," said Stella, sighing. She wrinkled her forehead in concentration. "Archery or the giant bungee trampoline... I think my brain would prefer the giant bungee trampoline."

"Good," said Grami. "Now ask yourself: 'Stella, would you prefer the giant bungee trampoline or the indoor skydiving?' Think carefully."

"I really *really* like jumping," said Stella.

"I never would have guessed," said Tad, teasingly.

Stella laughed and then said, "My brain and I choose the giant bungee trampoline!"

The other four *LM Club* members and their sponsor clapped for Stella, who said, "My brain *can* do this! I just didn't know how to give it only two options at a time." She was so excited she bounced up and down and up and down on her restaurant chair.

When they had finished eating lunch at *Mum's Munchies, Grami* announced, "It's time to meet our coaches. We need to obtain the proper protective equipment and begin our activities."

"The map shows that the archery and fencing activities are on the same side of the street," said Aimi. "Side by side."

"The giant bungee trampoline and indoor skydiving are next to each other, too, but on the other side of Main Street," said Toni.

"The Climbing Wall and Turtle Turf are at the very end of Main Street," Tad said. "That looks like quite a long way from here."

"It is a long way," said the waitress, who was busy clearing the dishes from the table. "But not to worry. An ET Transporter will take you there in no time at all."

Outside *Mum's Munchies* they met a tall young man holding a clip-board and a walkie-talkie. "Welcome," he

said. "Who chose the Rock Climbing Wall?" Tad waved an arm. "And who is visiting Turtle Turf?" Grami held up a hand. "Good," he said and then spoke into his walkie-talkie.

Soon an ET Transporter pulled up. The driver was a young

woman with a turtle emblem embroidered on her shirt. "Hop in, whoever needs a ride," she said. "Buckle up, and we'll be off. By the way, my name is Gaya, pronounced *Guy-ya.*"

Tad and Grami waved to the other *LM Club* members as they rode away in Gaya's ET Transporter.

"How high is the rock wall, *Guy-ya*?" asked Tad. "And did I say your name correctly?"

"You sure did," Gaya replied. "And the Rock Climbing Wall is approximately 50 feet high."

"That's more than 19 meters high," said Tad. "That's great! I was hoping for a high wall."

Main Street ended in a large Y-shaped driveway. Gaya turned into the right driveway and parked the cart. "We'll go in through those bright purple doors," said Gaya. "I want to make sure Ingrid is ready for you. Then I'll take Grami to Turtle Turf."

On the other side of the bright purple doors they met Ingrid, a tall blond girl with bright blue eyes and a beautiful smile. "You must be Tad," she said, smiling her beautiful smile. "I've been expecting you."

"Hello," said Tad, shaking hands. "I've wanted to try a Rock Climbing Wall forever, and I can hardly wait."

"Then let's get to it," Ingrid said, "although you don't look old enough to have a very long 'forever.' I'll have you climbing our new wall in nothing flat. Let's go into the equipment room so you can select a helmet, and I can outfit you with body pads and a safety harness. Do you have a favorite color, Tad?" she asked, waving her hand at a rack of helmets.

"Black, if you please," said Tad, pointing to a very shiny black helmet. "That one looks pretty *cool*."

"You have excellent taste," said Ingrid, taking the black shiny helmet from the rack and handing it to Tad. "The pads and the harness happen to be black, as well, so everything will match."

"You'll look quite *cool* on the DVD, Tad," said Gaya. "You're in good hands, too. Ingrid is the best climbing instructor we have. Enjoy yourself."

Gaya turned to Grami and, with a twinkle in her eye, said, "And you, young lady, are off to Turtle Turf."

They climbed into the ET Transporter. Gaya turned around and took the left side of the Y-shaped driveway. They drove through a long tunnel and stopped in a small parking lot. "Walk to that great green gate," Gaya told Grami. "That's where you'll meet your coach and get your safety equipment. Have fun with those centenarians."

Grami laughed. She could hear Gaya laughing, too, as she drove away.

Grami opened the great green gate and found herself inside a very large grassy enclosure with a lovely pond.

"Welcome to Turtle Turf," said a short pleasant-looking young woman. "I'm Twyla. How much do you know about turtles?"

"Not much," said Grami, "but I can learn and I am really looking forward to seeing your centenarians."

"I like that mindset," said Twyla, smiling broadly. "We have a couple land tortoises that are well over 100 years old. Here, pull on these over-boots and this is your walking stick. The ground is uneven in places and slippery in others. Oh, and here's your helmet. Falls are rare, but we'd like you to wear a helmet."

"Those are some pretty large looking rocks out there in the meadow," said Grami, pulling on a helmet that looked a little like a turtle shell.

"Those are a couple of centenarians," said Twyla, laughing, "and they do look like giant rocks from here."

"How old are they?" asked Grami.

"Well, let's just say that you are much *much* younger than they are," said Twyla, warming to her subject. "Those two are nearly 125 years old."

"Oh, my!" exclaimed Grami. "That's even older than some of the supercentenarians the LM Club members have been researching." And then Grami explained the definition of someone who is a supercentenarian: a person who has lived at least 110 years or longer.

"Amazing!" said Twyla. "Wow! Good for them! But other centenarian tortoises have lived even longer. Harriet, a resident at the Zoo in Queensland, Australia lived to be nearly 176 years old. Tu'i Malila reportedly lived with the Tongan royal family until it died of natural causes at the age of 188 years old."

"These are really Turtle Treasures," said Grami.

"Adwaita was a giant tortoise who lived at one of India's oldest zoological parks," said Twyla. "Adwaita may have lived at least 255 years. Oh, here is a bag of treats to feed our giant centenarians. I'll take pictures of you for the composite DVD that your group will take home. It will show clips of all six activities."

Grami opened the bag to see pieces of apple, banana, and vegetable pellets. "I'm ready to meet, greet, and feed these centenarians," said Grami, as she and Twyla crossed the meadow toward the two "rocks."

"Oh my!" Grami exclaimed. "They're huge! They are really humongous!" Twyla laughed and nodded.

Back at the fencing arena, Connor had been outfitted with a fencing uniform. It included ankle-length pants, a chest guard, and long-sleeved jacket. There were underarm protectors, socks, shoes with heel protectors, a  wire mesh mask with a padded bib to protect his neck, and a special large glove with extra padding for his weapon hand. A foil or point weapon completed his ensemble. "This is a complicated process," said Connor, holding the foil carefully. "It'll take a bit of getting used to what with all protective equipment."

The coach laughed. "It will. And it *is* a complicated process, which is why protective gear is important. Now, let's have a go at a fencing *bout* on a strip of ground or floor called a *piste*."

Next door in the archery arena, Aimi was wearing a complete stealth suit with a leather forearm protector, an archer tab to shield her fingers from the bowstring, and an archer helmet of leather and metal mesh, a bow, and a quiver containing six arrows.

"Oh, my goodness!" exclaimed Aimi, looking in the mirror. "I don't even recognize myself."

"Many people say that," said her archery coach, smiling. "Now, if you're ready, let's go to the archery hall."

Across Main Street, Stella was having the time of her life. Her coach had fitted Stella with a trampoline helmet and had buckled and clicked her into a bungee harness that would allow her to jump nearly 20 feet or almost 7 meters above the padded and net-enclosed giant bungee trampoline. Stella looked up and down.

"Ready?" asked her coach.

"Oh, yes!" cried Stella. "I *really* love jumping and this will be the most jumping fun ever. I'm so-o-o ready!"

At the Indoor Skydiving pavilion, Toni and her coach were dressed in skydiving outfits and helmets. If Grami and the other four *LM Club* members had not each been so busy with their own coaches and their own  activities, they might have seen Toni and her coach flying high on a cushion of air in the gigantic skydiving glass tube.

"I love this!" cried Toni. "I wish we had one of these at home. I'm sure this is way more fun than jumping out of an airplane and waiting for your parachute to open."

Her coach laughed. "If you're game, Toni, I'll turn up the air a smidgen, so we can fly even higher." Toni was game. Soon she and her coach flew higher and higher—and still higher.

When the activities were finally finished and the protective gear turned in, the ET Transporter picked everyone up and then dropped them off at *Mum's Munchies* for a snack of oatmeal-raisin bars and herb tea.

"Grami, I sure hope you had as much fun as I did," said Connor. "This was a great adventure. I think our school has a fencing club. Maybe I can join it next school year."

"I had a great time," said Grami. "I enjoyed meeting, greeting, and feeding those centenarian land tortoises, huge but gentle giants," said Grami. "You'll see them in the DVD." And then she told them about the 125-year-old *rocks*.

"Did you really think they were big rocks?" asked Aimi.

"Not really," said Grami, laughing. "But they did look like huge gray rocks from a distance." And then Grami repeated what Twyla had told her about the three very old land tortoises: Harriet, Tu'i Malila, and Adwaita.

"Maybe we can come here again next summer," said Aimi, "so I can see those centenarian land tortoises."

"My coach said I have a real knack for climbing," said Tad. "That's good news because I love it. There's a rock climbing wall at the community center. I'm going to ask my dad if we can climb together."

"I bet our dad would go with you, too!" exclaimed Toni. "He used to rock climb in college, you know. Maybe you've inherited some of his skills."

"Rock climbing is my new favorite," said Tad. "Followed by rabbits and riddles. And Grami's sandwiches, of course."

"And writing verses?" asked Grami.

"Oh, verses," said Tad. "Definitely. Verses are my fifth favorite."

"I'm choosing archery as my physical-education class when school starts again," said Aimi. "I got close to the bull's eye several times today, and my coach told me that was pretty good for my first hands-on lesson."

Just then the receptionist brought their DVD. "Enjoy it," she said.

"Oh, we will," cried Stella, taking the DVD. "We will enjoy it! Thank you."

Five *LM Club* members and their sponsor went out to the parking lot, got into Grami's car, and belted up.

"Let's go straight home and look at the DVD," said Toni. "I can hardly wait for you to see how much fun Stella and I had when you watch her on the giant bungee trampoline and watch me in the gigantic skydiving glass tube—floating on air, no less!"

"I sure hope they took good pictures of me during the fencing activity," said Connor. "*On point,* and all that, because I want my folks to see all my protective gear."

"Hey, Tad," said Toni. "You look like you're day dreaming. Are you?"

Tad smiled. "I am. I learned today how much I like rock climbing. I can hardly wait to get home and, after Dad sees the DVD, talk to him about rock climbing."

"What did you all learn today?" asked Grami.

"That there are many fun activities that could be dangerous without appropriate protective equipment," said Connor.

"I learned my brain *can* choose one thing," said Stella, "even if I thought it couldn't."

"Jazzercise has always been my favorite sport" said Toni. "Today was so mega-*cool* that I just might like to be an indoor skydiving coach."

"I'd like to watch the DVD first thing," said Aimi. "I want to see what each person did."

"I learned how hungry rock climbing made me," said Tad. "I think we should eat first!"

"Let's do both," said Grami. "Watch the DVD and eat. Yes, you've all expended a huge amount of energy."

"I sure did," said Conner, "and Tad is always hungry anyway."

"Well, I'm doubly hungry today," said Tad. "I hope our sponsor fixed a lot of food!"

"Your *LM Club* sponsor did just that," said Grami, smiling. "First I'll turn on the DVD and then we can dig in."

And that's exactly what they did.

Early to bed and early to rise,
Help you stay both healthy and wise.
Shut-eye myths be sure to quell—
Cuz living long means sleeping well.

9—Elusive Shuteye

"Grami," said Aimi, clicking the candy red cell phone closed, "Tad, Toni, and Connor will be here at 10 o'clock. Their practicing will be finished and they'll have a jacket, walking shoes, and sunglasses."

"Great," said Grami, smiling.

"They wanted to know what adventure the Longevity Mystery Club sponsor—that's you, Grami—had planned this time," said Stella.

"And what did you tell them?" asked Grami.

"That the LMC sponsor likes to keep the adventures a surprise," said Stella, laughing. "

"Many adventures need walking shoes, a jacket, and sunglasses," said Aimi. "There's no point in trying to guess what the adventure is going to be."

"No point at all," said Grami, smiling.

"Can Buddy-the-Beagle come?" asked Stella.

Grami shook her head.

"Then I guess we're not going to the park," Stella said. "I'll play with Buddy-the-Beagle in the back yard for a while. Maybe he won't feel so bad when we leave."

"He may be lonesome for a short time," said Grami, "but he'll soon fall asleep, and then Buddy-the-Beagle will be very happy to see you tonight."

At two minutes before ten o'clock the doorbell chimed—and then chimed again.

"Someone is in a big hurry for this adventure to begin," said Stella to no one in particular as she opened the

131

front door. Tad, Toni, and Connor tumbled into the room. "Come in," cried Stella. "Do come in."

"We're already in," said Connor, laughing.

"Aimi, did you find out where we're going on this adventure?" asked Tad.

"Not yet," said Aimi, "but Grami just told Stella that Buddy-the-Beagle will be happy to see her *tonight*. That means it's either a long adventure or quite far away."

"Hello, detectives," said Grami, coming into the room with her jacket, car keys, and dark glasses. "You are on time and all ready. It's a pleasure being your sponsor."

"We have walking shoes, jackets, and sun glasses," said Toni.

"And each of us has a *My Sleuth Notebook*," said Connor. "We are prepared. You know I like to be prepared."

"Well, in that case," said Grami, "since everyone is prepared, let us be on our way."

"The back door is already ajar," said Aimi, picking up her jacket.

"The back door is not a *jar*," said Connor. "The back door is a door."

"Good one, Connor," Aimi said, laughing.

"Look at the piles of boards in the back yard!" Stella exclaimed, as they walked toward the car. "Those boards had not yet been delivered when you were here two days ago. Piles of boards in the back yard are exciting because they spell *treehouse!*"

"Actually, they spell boards, b-o-a-r-d-s," said Tad.

Stella laughed and rolled her eyes." You are teasing me again, Tad," she said. "But I don't mind anymore."

"The piles of boards are quality supplies for the LMC treehouse," said Grami. "Now, climb in and buckle up. The first part of today's adventure begins at the Neo-Leo Wordpark. We'll spend thirty minutes investigating human sleep and another thirty minutes researching sleep

in non-human mammals."

"That's exciting!" said Tad,

"What's exciting?" asked Connor. "The piles of boards in Grami's back yard or the research on sleep?"

"Both," said Tad, punching Connor in the arm.

A few minutes later Grami parked the car and they climbed the steps to the Neo-Leo Wordpark, past the two huge crouching cement lions, and in through the wide front door. They all headed for the rows of computers.

Sixty minutes later, Grami said, "All right, sleuths. The hour is up. Time for part two of today's adventure." Gathering their belongings, the five LMC members and their sponsor went back to the car.

"How long will it take to get there?" asked Tad.

"A couple hours," said Grami. "I have lunch for us to eat in the trunk before we start the adventure."

"Are we eating in the trunk?" asked Stella, a puzzled look on her face. "I want to *know*."

"I have lunch for us to eat *and* it's in the brown wicker basket in the trunk," said Grami, laughing.

"Your lunches are healthier now, Grami," said Tad. "They're even tastier than the ones you used to make, and I don't seem to get hungry as quickly as I used to."

"That's because healthier foods don't spike your blood sugar like unhealthier ones do," said Toni. "Since it doesn't shoot up so high it doesn't fall down so low."

"And that means you're more likely to feel hungry when your body really needs food rather than due to low blood sugar. Shall we debrief as we drive?" asked Grami.

"Remind me again what de-breef means," said Stella. "Somebody tell me. I want to *know*."

"Who can answer Stella's question?" asked Grami.

"I think I know what it means," said Tad, "but I'm not sure I can explain it clearly. Would you do it?"

"In the military and in other organizations, as well," said Grami, "when a commanding officer receives reports about a mission or the president of a company receives reports about products or services it's called debriefing."

"So, our club sponsor is going to receive reports from the five LMC sleuths," said Toni.

"Who debriefs first?" Stella asked. "I want to *know*!"

"Let's go alphabetically by first name," said Grami. "Tell us something new you learned about human sleep and about non-human mammals and their sleep."

Aimi opened her *Notebook*. "It takes longer to recover from mental work than physical work," she read. "I did not *know* that! Adults need seven to nine hours and kids need eight to ten hours of sleep a day." She paused. "Armadillos sleep eighteen hours a day. Wow!"

"You spend about a third of your life sleeping," said Connor. "In the US there are 100,000 vehicle accidents annually due to driver drowsiness. In terms of reaction time, after 20 hours without sleep, the brain is functioning at the level of a brain that has reached the legal limit of alcohol intoxication in California. Chimpanzees sleep nearly ten hours and cats almost thirteen hours a day."

"Do you know what I discovered?" asked Stella. "S comes after C and before T."

"Is that what you discovered?" asked Aimi.

"No," said Stella, laughing. "I learned that sleep is in-de-pen-dent-ly linked with longevity. And that people who don't get enough sleep often gain weight. Grami, did you not get enough sleep? Is that why you got obese? Are you getting enough sleep now? I want to *know*!"

"That's three questions," said Grami, smiling. "The three answers are, *no*, *probably*, and *yes*."

"Dogs sleep about ten hours a day," said Stella. "I know Buddy-the-Beagle sleeps at least ten hours, but some days he also howls for an hour. I wonder if he really thinks he's singing?" No one answered her question.

"When you lose sleep, your brain can get very irritable," said Tad. "If your brain hasn't had time to finish all the repair work it needs to do while you were sleeping, you can develop health problems and have trouble learning and remembering."

"I also looked up elephants," said Connor, "and learned that in some countries, elephant rides are big business—but they're not good for their back."

"Really," said Grami. "I didn't *know* that."

"Some guides who sit on the elephant's neck use a heavy wooden chair for the riders and the elephant's back can begin to sag painfully or even break," said Connor.

"That's horrible!" exclaimed Aimi. "Don't the guides realize that?"

"One would hope so," said Grami. "But when people are trying to earn a living, a popular tourist attraction is a way to make money. Guides may be so busy trying to make ends meet on their salary that they may not think about how the elephant's back is being harmed."

"That's so sad," said Toni, indignantly. "I will never ride on an elephant in a heavy wooden chair!" She paused. "Well, I learned that tigers sleep for nearly sixteen hours a day, while giraffes may sleep for about thirty minutes. Only thirty minutes! Can you beat that?"

"I beat that every night," said Connor. "And I'm

pretty sure I have done so every night of my life so far."

"Personally, Connor, I had no idea giraffes needed so little sleep," said Grami. "And I agree with you, Toni. I never plan to ride on an elephant in a heavy wooden chair, either." The other four LMC members nodded their agreement.

"Your turn to debrief, Grami," said Aimi.

"I discovered that while you are asleep, your brain works harder than when you are awake. It repairs cells and tries to solve problems that might have puzzled you during the day. After a good night's sleep, you may find an answer more easily the next morning. Your creativity might be improved, too," said Grami.

"Debriefing is fun," said Stella, clapping her hands.

"I'm glad Tad and Connor researched elephants," said Grami, "because here we are at the second part of our adventure." She turned the car into a wide driveway and stopped in front of a boom gate. A young man wearing a green uniform and a hat with a logo on it was standing beside the boom gate.

"Welcome to Pachyderm Paradise. Did you bring a lunch to eat?" asked the young man. "Many do."

"We did," said Grami. "And some in our group are ready to eat."

"Park by that gray building," he told Grami. "You can watch a DVD about elephants while you eat your lunch in the pavilion." The young man slipped a parking permit under one of the car's windshield wipers. "When you're done eating," he continued, "walk through that red turnstile over there and meet your guide." The boom gate raised and Grami drove through the entrance and parked beside the gray pavilion."

"What is a pak-i-derm?" asked Stella. "Does it have something to do with travel or a suitcase? I want to *know*."

"Elephants are sometimes called pachyderms," said Grami, smiling. "It's a rehabilitation farm, a sanctuary for sick elephants that were left behind by a traveling circus or were orphaned when their mother died. Perhaps some of the elephants may have an injured back from giving people rides. I thought you'd like to do elephant research in person and not just on the Internet. You'll be able to feed some of the pachyderms here, too."

"Wow!" exclaimed Tad. "Thank you, Grami."

"Am I too little to feed an elephant?" asked Stella, looking very concerned. "I was too little to go on the new 'Red-Roller' ride at the Turvy-Topsy Amusement Park. Will I be too little to feed an elephant? I want to *know*."

"I called ahead and asked that very question," said Grami. "I was assured that there are a couple of little elephants that our littlest detective can feed."

"Goody-goody!" cried Stella. She was so excited she clapped her hands, jumped up in the air, and twirled three times.

"Good thing Connor and I are carrying the brown wicker basket," said Tad. "You might have dropped our lunch with all your clapping and jumping and twirling."

"More teasing!" said Stella, but she smiled.

When Tad and Connor had carried the brown wicker basket into the gray pavilion and set it on a table, Grami pointed to a large screen. "The sign by the clock says the next showing starts in three minutes. This is good timing. Let's see what new things we can learn."

Thirty minutes later both the DVD and lunch were finished. There were no leftovers.

Tad and Connor put the now-empty brown wicker basket in the trunk. Then the five sleuths and their sponsor walked through the red turnstile where they were met by another young man who was also wearing a green uniform and a hat with a logo on it. "Welcome," he said smiling. "My name is Hari, and I will be your personal elephant guide."

"We are members of the Longevity Mystery Club," said Stella. "Detectives, actually."

"And Grami is our club sponsor," said Aimi.

Hari bowed respectfully to Grami.

"We also have a club mascot," said Stella. "But Buddy-the-Beagle did not come with us."

"That was a good choice," said Hari. "If a little beagle was running around underfoot, maybe even howling, the elephants might get nervous."

"Grami says that pak-i-derm is another name for an elephant," said Stella.

"Correct," said Hari. "It comes from a Greek word meaning *thick skin*. An elephant's skin can be up to an inch or two and a half centimeters thick."

"The DVD said their skin is very sensitive to touch," said Toni. "And that's the reason they spray themselves with water or roll in the mud or dust to help protect their skin from sunburns and biting insects."

"You listen carefully," said Hari.

"We all do," said Aimi. "We like to learn things and solve mysteries. Listening carefully is important."

"It certainly is," agreed Hari. "We'll take this path toward the elephant feeding ground. While we walk you can tell me what else you learned from the DVD."

"I learned that African elephants have large ears in the shape of the African continent," said Connor. "Both males and females have tusks. Their skin is very wrinkly. And it's like they have two fingers at the end of their trunk to help them pick up things."

"Yes," said Hari, "and the back of the African

elephant is a little bit swayed. You will see some African elephants here. In fact, we have two babies whose mothers died." Hari looked at Stella and smiled. "I think you will be just the right size to feed them."

Stella started to clap her hands, jump up in the air and twirl—but stopped herself just in the nick of time.

"What's the other type of elephant?" asked Hari.

"Asian elephants," said Aimi. "They have small ears and only the males have tusks. Their backs are dome-shaped, and they only have one finger-like thing at the end of their trunk."

"Well done," said Hari, nodding. "What else?"

"Bush elephants eat grass and flowering plants, bushes, and even small trees," said Tad.

"Forest elephants also eat fruit and seeds. They can eat five percent of their weight every day."

"Our elephants eat a little less than that," said Hari. "That's because they don't have to use so many calories searching for food. But African elephants are the largest mammals on land, so an adult male still needs to eat about seventy thousand calories and drink up to fifty gallons of water a day, depending on the temperature of the air."

"I was surprised to learn that elephants have a built-in air conditioner," said Grami. "When they flap their wet ears on a hot day, blood flowing through blood vessels in their ears is cooled, which helps keep their bodies cooler."

"Yes," said Hari. "Elephants carry their own built-in air conditioner with them. Very handy, I must say."

"That would be very handy on a hot day," said Tad.

"Did you know that just as etiquette can be important in human society, it is also important in elephant society?" asked Hari.

"What is et-i-cut?" asked Stella. "Did someone get cut or hurt? I want to *know*."

Hari looked at Grami. "How would *you* explain etiquette, Grami?" he asked.

"Well," said Grami, "let me think for a minute." They all walked along the path with Hari in silence while Grami was thinking. Finally Grami said, "Etiquette involves a set of rules that tells individuals in a group or society or culture the type of behaviors that are socially acceptable. For example, when you meet someone for the first time, do you shake hands, rub noses, pump fists, or bow?"

"Rub noses!" cried Stella. "I do not want to rub noses. Who would want to rub noses? I want to *know*."

"Probably elephants," said Connor, laughing. "Their noses are big enough, that's for sure."

"We can talk about social and cultural etiquette on the way home, Stella," said Grami. "Right now, I want to know what Hari can tell us about elephant etiquette."

"Thank you, Grami," said Hari, keeping his face straight with some difficulty. "Now, let's apply your explanation to the life of elephants. They exhibit specific behaviors when they relate to others in the herd. For example, trunks are used in greeting. A lower-ranking animal will insert its trunk tip into the mouth of a higher-ranking elephant. A trunk may be held out to an approaching elephant as a greeting or used to caress other family members, especially baby elephant calves."

"The DVD said an elephant's trunk is both a nose and a hand," said Stella. "How can it be both a nose and a hand? I want to *know*."

"Elephants use their trunk much like you use your hands," said Hari, "to pick up or grab and hold, to reach, touch, pull, push, and throw. There are no bones or cartilage in an elephant's trunk, but it is so strong it can push down entire trees. On the other hand, the trunk is so agile it can pick up a single piece of straw. Imagine that!"

"But an elephant's trunk cannot clap," said Stella. Tad and Connor laughed out loud.

"No, it cannot clap," said Hari smiling. "But their trunk is a nose, too. They use it to smell and breathe. The two nostrils suck air up into the lungs. They use their trunk to drink, too, but they suck water only part way up the trunk. Then they curl it toward their mouth, tilt their head up, and let the water pour into their mouth."

"Oh-h-h-h," whispered Stella, as they turned a corner in the path. "Do you see what I see?" Half a dozen adult elephants were standing in a field beside a large pool of water—right in front of the visitors. "They are so big!" said Stella, taking Grami's hand.

"That they are," said Hari, chuckling. "We call that large pool of water Elephant Bay. But look over here." He pointed to a small enclosure off to one side where two little elephant calves were looking over the log fence. Each was a little over a meter (about three feet) tall, quite hairy, with a long tail and a very short trunk. "These are just your size, Stella," said Hari. "You can feed them if you like."

A baby-elephant nurse showed Stella how to bottle-feed an elephant calf.

"Look, Grami," said Stella. "The baby elephant is leaning against my arm. I think it likes me."

"It definitely likes you," said the baby-elephant nurse. "What's not to like?" Stella smiled. She fed a bottle of formula to the first baby elephant. Then she gave a bottle to the second baby elephant. "I just love feeding these baby elephants, Grami," Stella whispered. "Can I stay here for a while?"

"Stay here as long as you want," said Hari. "I'll take the others to feed the larger elephants." The adolescent and adult elephants enjoyed the celery, lettuce, cucumbers, and herbivore pellets the visitors offered them.

"What is that sound?" asked Connor, looking around the field of elephants. "I don't recognize it."

"Elephant stomach growls," said Hari.

"I don't think stomach growls would be considered good etiquette in our society," said Toni, laughing.

"They are good etiquette in elephant society," said Hari. "Stomach growls seem to be a signal to the other elephants that everything is *A-Okay*."

"The DVD said that elephants make trumpeting sounds, too," said Aimi.

"Yes," said Hari. "The sound can be as loud as 117 decibels and may travel distances up to six miles. Make that 60 or 70 years for the average elephant. Elephants also use low-frequency *infrasounds* that are lower than the normal limit of human hearing, but which you can often sense or feel," Hari continued. Infrasounds are used to coordinate the movement of herds and allow mating elephants to find each other. These special sounds can travel through solid ground and be sensed by other elephants using their feet, even when the herds are separated by hundreds of  miles. Elephants have better low-frequency infrasound hearing than any other mammal tested so far."

The time flew by. The LM Club members took turns feeding the elephant calves, the adolescents, and even the adults, and took pictures standing beside them. One very tame female elephant let them sit on her trunk, one at a time, and raised them up a little bit off the ground.

When Grami finally thought to check her watch, it was almost closing time for the Pachyderm Paradise.

"Come again any time," said Hari. "The elephants obviously like you and feel comfortable around you. Next time maybe you can bring your bathing suits and help me scrub these pachyderms in Elephant Bay."

"That sounds like a good idea," said Grami. "After all, who gets to give an elephant a bath?"

"That was a wonderful adventure!" said Aimi, as they climbed into the car. "Thank you, Grami." The other LMC members thanked Grami, too.

"I wrote a new verse," said Tad. "It goes like this:
Pachyderm Paradise at Elephant Bay,
Was amazing in every possible way.
We learned that infrasounds are low,
And help a mate to find its beau.

"I like that verse, Tad," said Grami, turning onto the highway. "It was amazing in every possible way. Remember, you're all staying at my house tonight. And feel free to nap on the way home."

"Except for you," said Stella, yawning sleepily.

"Except for me," agreed Grami. "Someone has to drive the car. I think Toni and Aimi are already asleep and Tad and Stella are not far behind."

"I'll stay awake and keep you company," said Connor. "That's the least I can do. We can talk about Pachyderms, infrasounds, and etiquette. And about coming back to help Hari scrub the elephants."

And that's exactly what they did

Creatures that fly or those who hang glide,
Must be most careful not to collide.
Birds on the wing may soar the skies—
There's only one mammal that truly flies.

10—20:80 Magic

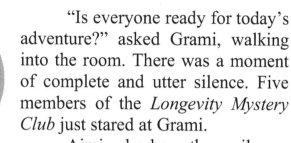

"Is everyone ready for today's adventure?" asked Grami, walking into the room. There was a moment of complete and utter silence. Five members of the *Longevity Mystery Club* just stared at Grami.

Aimi broke the silence. "Grami! You are wearing slacks! Wow! You look great!"

"Wow is right," said Toni. "Here's looking at you!"

One look and Stella was so excited that she clapped her hands, jumped up in the air, and twirled three times.

"Good job!" cried Tad and Connor, clapping their hands. Aimi and Toni clapped, too. Grami did not clap her hands, jump up in the air or twirl three times, but she looked quite pleased.

"Your Weekly Comparison Form on the cork board above your computer was correct," said Stella. "Your BMI is lower, your waist size is smaller, and you weigh less—*and* you're wearing slacks!"

"Did Grami's Weekly Comparison Form say she was wearing slacks?" asked Tad, a twinkle in his eye.

"No!" exclaimed Stella, laughing. "But I am excited because I want Grami to live to be a centenarian. No, wait! I want her to live to be a very very *very* old su-per-cen-ten-ar-ian!"

"Thank you for noticing," said Grami, when she had stopped laughing. "I feel much better. I have more energy. And I am now able to fit into a pair of slacks that have been hanging in my closet for a long time. I believe they'll fill the bill for today's adventure."

At that, everyone started talking at once asking questions about the adventure. "We'll spend an hour at the Neo-Leo Wordpark to research some non-human creatures that fly or glide. Then we'll move on to part two of our adventure," said Grami.

"What non-human creatures?" asked Stella. "I want to *know*.

"I've selected five categories," said Grami. "Bats, fish, frogs, snakes, and squirrels."

"I'll take bats," said Connor, immediately.

"Fish for me," said Aimi. "I never heard of *flying* fish, but I'll see what I can discover."

"I've not heard of a *flying* snake," said Tad, "but I know Grami. She wouldn't have that category if there was nothing to sleuth. Snakes it is."

"I like squirrels," said Stella. "I've heard of *flying* squirrels, so I'll research them."

"That leaves frogs," said Toni. "*Flying* frogs? That sounds like a ride at the Turvy-Topsy Amusement Park." She started to laugh. "Oh, this will be fun."

"Grami, I've been thinking," said Stella.

"Uh-oh. That could be very dangerous," said Tad, chuckling.

"Well, I *have* been thinking," said Stella, saucily. "I think we need to shop for new clothes for you, Grami."

"Give me a few more weeks," said Grami. "Maybe I'll get a new outfit when the *LM Club* treehouse is finished."

"Good idea," said Stella. "Something really snazzy for the celebration, you know."

"Speaking of celebration, when can we have one?" asked Aimi.

"When Grami gets new clothes?" asked Stella.

"No, for our *LM Club* treehouse opening," said Aimi.

"And will *you* cut the ribbon, Grami, like they did at the Neo-Leo Wordpark?" asked Connor.

"After all, you *are* the *Club* sponsor," said Toni.

"Plus the big tree is in *your* back yard," said Tad.

"That would be an honor," said Grami. "Let's think about it. Right now, however, collect your jackets, sunglasses, and *My Sleuth Notebook*s. It's time we were on our way."

"For the *first* part of this adventure," said Tad.

Grami drove them to the Neo-Leo Wordpark and parked the car. Soon the five *LM Club* members and their sponsor were each busy at a computer—sleuthing.

An hour later, when Grami checked her watch, she said, "It's time for part two of our adventure."

"Time went by very fast today," said Tad.

"Time went by at the same speed it always does," said Connor. "You were just more interested today."

"Thanks for that important bit of information," said Tad, laughing. "I suppose you're probably right. By the way, Grami, you've not told us where we're going for part two of today's *LM Club* adventure."

"Let's debrief first," said Grami, driving out of the parking lot and heading for the highway. "I start. Maybe that will give you a clue and help you guess where we're going." Tad nodded.

"I looked up formations that are often found in caves or caverns," said Grami, "and learned an easy way to remember which formation is which. Stalactites hold *tight* to the ceiling. Their name contains a 'c' for *ceiling*. Stalagmites grow from the ground upward due to the accumulation of dripping water. Their name has a 'g' for *ground*."

"I can remember that," said Stella. "The word *stalactite* has a 'c' for ceiling because stalactites hang down from the ceiling. The word *stalagmite* has a 'g' for ground because stalagmites grow up from the ground.

They grow from dripping water." She clapped her hands and would have jumped up in the air and twirled three times, but her seatbelt held her in place.

"Connor, you're next. You researched bats, if I recall correctly," said Grami.

"You do," said Connor. Recall correctly. I discovered there are 1,240 species of bats. Some are *mega* bats—or flying foxes—with a wingspan of about three feet or one meter, and they like to roost in trees. *Micro* bats are much smaller and prefer to live in caves or buildings."

"Wow!" Toni exclaimed. "1, 240 species!"

Connor smiled at Toni and then continued. "Bats eat mostly insects, which they find by using echolocation. They are the only mammals capable of true, sustained flight. Their forelimbs form webbed wings, and they flap long spread-out fingers that are covered with a thin skin called a *patagium.*"

"Pa-tay-gee-um," interrupted Stella.

"As I was saying," continued Connor, glancing pointedly at Stella, "all other non-human creatures *glide* for short distances, except for birds, of course."

"Stalactites, stalagmites, and bats," said Aimi, thoughtfully. "Grami, are we going to the Krystal Kaverns? Our teacher told us about them."

"Good guess, Aimi," said Grami. "We are, and while we are driving you can debrief about flying fish."

"Fish don't really *fly*," said Aimi. "Not like birds. They leap into the air out of warm water oceans all over the world. Wing-like fins help them glide just above the surface for distances of between 600 and 1200 feet (180-365 meters). There are about 40 known species of flying fish and all have unevenly forked tails."

"Flying snakes don't really *fly*, either," said Tad, chuckling. "The Paradise tree snake's slim body, for example, is about three feet long. It has no wings and no engine, something like a glider. But its gliding ability is considered one of the best among flying snakes. They can glide up to thirty-two feet (ten meters), between trees."

Tad paused, turned a page in his *My Sleuth Notebook,* and continued. "I discovered that their black bodies are covered in rich green scales. Some also have clusters of red, orange, and yellow scales that look

151

something like flowers running in a line down their backs from the base of their necks to their tails. I'd sure like to see one of those Paradise tree snakes."

"Which brings us to flying frogs," said Grami, smiling at both Tad and Toni in the rear-view mirror.

"Well," said Toni, glancing at her *My Sleuth Notebook,* "Grami was correct. There *are* flying frogs. Some of the largest are the Wallace parachute frogs. The skin between their toes and loose skin flaps along their sides catch the air and help them glide for 50 feet (15 meters) or more. They live in the dense jungles of Malaysia  and Borneo and spend most of their time gliding from tree to tree. They can leap from a branch and 'splay' or spread out their four webbed feet. Their oversized toe pads help them land softly and stick to a neighboring tree trunk. It would be fun to watch them."

"My turn," said Stella. "Flying squirrels are a type of tet-ra-pod. That means they are animals with four feet, you know," she said, importantly. "Squirrels don't really *fly,* either. They just glide between trees." She waved her arms about in a gliding motion.

"Watch it, little sister," said Aimi, laughing. "Maybe you better wait to demonstrate gliding until we are out of the car."

"Flying squirrels have parachute-like skin that stretches between their two arms and legs; a *pa-tag-eum* like bats," Stella went on, completely ignoring Aimi's comment. "And guess what? Flying squirrels can change their speed and direction while they are gliding in mid-air just by changing the position of their arms and legs. The Internet said that their fluffy tails act like an air-brake, helping them land safely on a tree trunk or branch. *And they're capable of gliding up to 295 feet (90 meters) on one flight.*" Stella paused as she closed her *My Sleuth Notebook.* "I had no idea there were nearly four dozen different types of squirrels!"

"We are learning so much this summer," said Aimi. "Next year in school I'll have lots of things in mind to choose from when we're asked to write about something."

"And here we are at the Krystal Kaverns," said Grami, turning into a large parking lot and stopping the car. "Grab your jackets. It may be cold inside."

"Welcome to the Krystal Kaverns," said the middle-aged man in a uniform who greeted them behind the counter in the lobby of the Krystal Kaverns Lodge. "My name is Ethan. How many are in your party, please?"

"Six, Sir," said Toni, promptly. "Five members of the *Longevity Mystery Club* and Grami, *Club* sponsor."

"Will we see stal-ac-tites with a 'c' for ceiling and stal-ag-mi-tes with a 'g' for ground?" asked Stella.

"What about bats? Are there any bats inside the Krystal Kaverns?" asked Connor, excitedly. "We've been studying non-human creatures that fly or glide. My topic was bats. I learned that bats are the only mammals that are capable of true, sustained flight."

"Yes and yes," said Ethan, smiling. "Methinks I have some walking encyclopedias on my tour today. I also see that you have jackets and sturdy walking shoes." Ethan winked at Grami and smiled. "Someone in this group was thinking ahead. Six plus one—the one being me—equals seven people on this tour."

Grami took out her credit card and paid the entrance fees for the five *LM Club* members and their sponsor.

Ethan strapped on a headlamp and hooked a walkie-talkie on his belt. "Let's get going," he said. Unlocking a door in the Lodge wall behind the counter, Ethan stepped

through the doorway into a tunnel that sloped slightly downward. It was just high enough so Ethan did not hit his head on the ceiling. "Right this way. Follow me. And mind your head."

"That won't be a problem for us," said Connor to Tad, snickering. "Not yet, anyway. We're way shorter than Ethan."

A rope railing ran on either side of the narrow path. After what seemed quite a long way, the tunnel suddenly opened into a huge natural cave-room. At the end of the path, a very long flight of steps went down and down and still further down. Everyone stopped and looked around.

"Amazing," whispered Grami. "I'd forgotten how grand the Krystal Kaverns really are!"

"Stalactites. Wow!" breathed Toni.

"Stalagmites! Double wow!" Aimi whispered.

"Are we supposed to whisper?" asked Tad. "I didn't see a sign that said to whisper."

"How come the names start with 'K' instead of 'C?'" asked Aimi, before Ethan could answer Tad.

Ethan laughed. "You're more likely to remember a name with unusual spelling. And people often whisper when they first step into this enormous cave-room. Some think it looks like a magnificent cathedral with formations that resemble carved statues and a pipe organ."

Single file, the six tourists and their guide carefully descended the stairway. "I counted 47 steps," said Connor. "That was *very* long stairway."

"Yes," said Ethan. "We are now about three stories underground. Look ahead." He stepped to the side of the path. "We will continue to follow this sloping path down at least another story or two. Everybody ready?" The six tourists nodded.

As they walked along the path, Ethan pointed out one interesting formation after another. Electric light bulbs strung above the path helped give some light. The light on Ethan's headband acted like a spot-light when he pointed it toward one formation after another. "This next section of path is a bit steeper," Ethan told the group. "It's also damp because of dripping water." He shone his headlight down the path. "Look ahead. We'll be crossing a 'hog back' that rises above a stream in the  bottom of this cavern. Whatever you do, *don't slip and fall.* I tell you, it's a very very long way down if you slip and fall!"

No sooner had Ethan started down the path with the six tourists following him, when Aimi suddenly slipped and fell. "Help!" she cried. "Somebody help me!"

Toni screamed with fright. Grami reached for Aimi and luckily grabbed a handful of her thick hair.

Ethan came pounding back up the path and helped Grami pull Aimi to safety. "I told you to *be careful*!" he said in a big loud voice. Crying, Aimi buried her face in Grami's side.

"Excuse me, Sir," said Tad, respectfully. "I believe you said, '*Don't slip and fall.*'"

"That's exactly what I said," snapped Ethan." Same difference."

"Grami says there *is* a difference," said Connor. "When you say, '*Don't* do something,' your brain creates a picture of the something you don't want to do."

"Aimi," said Stella, holding her sister's hand, "did you see a picture of yourself slipping in your mind's eye?" Aimi nodded, her face still buried in Grami's side.

"What in the world are they talking about?" asked Ethan, puzzled and looking at Grami.

"Words create mental pictures in your brain," said Grami. "It deals easily with positives—a one-step process that tells you what to do. But negatives are a two-step process and more difficult. The brain may miss the 'don't' and follow the first picture. For example, if I say, 'Don't think about the white bear,' what do you see in your mind's eye?"

"Oh, my goodness," said Ethan. "I see a white bear in my mind's eye. Who knew?"

Ethan knelt beside Aimi, now sitting on the path.

"I apologize for speaking so loudly, young lady. Well, shouting, really. Your slip and fall scared me, but that's no excuse. Tell me what I should say another time."

Aimi wiped the tears from her eyes. "You could tell your brain what to do by saying this: Walk carefully, stay on the path, and hold onto the rope."

Ethan nodded. "Simple enough. Walk carefully. Stay on the path. Hold onto the rope. Good. How fortunate that you were on my tour today," he said. "Knowing this

can help me be a better tour guide, and if you hadn't slipped I would never have learned this brain stuff."

"Grami says good things can come out of bad things," said Aimi, in her soft sweet voice. "So all is well that ends well."

"You're trembling," said Ethan. "Are you cold Aimi? I can give you my jacket."

Aimi shook her head but kept on trembling. "When the brain experiences a shock," Grami explained, "it triggers the stress response and pours out stress hormones like adrenalin and cortisol. After the shock, the muscles tremble to release the no-longer needed energy. She'll stop shaking when her muscles are ready."

"Grami," said Aimi in a rather small voice. "I'm afraid I will slip again."

"Take a deep breath, Aimi," said Grami. "Hold it for a moment and blow it out slowly through pursed lips." Aimi did. "Now, change your self-talk. Tell your brain what you want to have happen."

"Oh, right," said Aimi. "I mean, correct. Okay." She took a deep breath. "Aimi, you are walking safely on the path. You are holding Grami's hand. You're glad to be at the Krystal Kaverns."

Ethan watched carefully. "Aimi," he said, "your muscles just stopped trembling! It's like magic. I guess I have a lot *yet* to learn."

"Do you have a computer?" asked Toni. "Grami takes us to the Neo-Leo Wordpark, and we research stuff on the Internet. You could do that, too."

"What is the Neo-Leo Wordpark?" asked Ethan.

"It's our new 21st century library," said Stella, "and it has a Librivox Zone and two crouching lions."

"I certainly hope the two crouching lions are made of cement," said Ethan, chuckling. "A Librivox Zone?" He raised a rather bushy eyebrow.

Grami told him about the new 21st century building with free Wi-Fi and many computers. She described the two crouching *cement* lions and explained the Librivox Zone. "I had to learn to stop whispering when we are at the Neo-Leo Wordpark," she told him, laughing.

"Once when I was a boy," said Ethan, "the librarian asked me to leave because she said my whispering was too loud. I like the idea of a Librivox Zone. No whispering required. That would work for me."

"I'm ready now," whispered Aimi, standing up and holding Grami's hand. "I remembered the 20:80 Rule."

"Excellent!" said Ethan, standing up and clapping his hands.

"Oh! I hear clapping!" cried Stella. "Are other tourists here? I want to *know*!"

Ethan shook his head. "Echoes," he said. "I'll clap again. Listen carefully." After the last faint echo had died away, Ethan spoke again. "By way of apology for my, ah-h, speaking so loudly and scaring Aimi, I have decided to let you see a very special area in the Krystal Kaverns that is not usually open to tourists."

A few hundred feet farther down the path, Ethan unhooked a portion of the rope handrail and carefully led the six sightseers off the path toward a wrought-iron gate  set into the cave wall. When they reached the wrought-iron gate, Ethan took a ring of keys from his belt. Selecting one, he unlocked the gate. They walked through the opening into a short tunnel that led to another cave-room. Although smaller across, it was very high up.

"Oh!" cried Stella. "This cave-room has a sky light!"

"It's a natural sky light, opening to the outside," said Ethan. "I'll turn off my headlamp. When your eyes adjust to the darkness, tell me what you see." He turned off the light and waited.

"I see some shapes moving around," said Toni.

"Bats! Are they bats?" asked Connor excitedly.

"That's exactly what they are," said Ethan. "Thousands and thousands of bats."

"I've been reading about bats," said Conner. "Are these mega bats or mini echolocation bats?"

"Why, echolocation bats, young man," said Ethan, obviously surprised. "You have been studying." They watched for a long time and talked about bats and echolocation and stalactites and stalagmites and other wonders in the Krystal Kaverns. Finally, they made their way back through the short tunnel to the wrought-iron gate, then along the path to the very long stairway, and finally back up to the lodge.

"The cafeteria has a meal all ready for our group," said Ethan. "Come this way." When he and the six tourists were seated at a round table, and the waitress had brought their food, Ethan said, "Aimi, you said something about a 20:80 Rule. What *is* that?"

"It's what Grami calls the Stress Equation," replied Aimi. "Grami, you explain it to him. Please."

"Stressors are believed to interact with the brain in a two-part equation, sometimes referred to as the 20:80 Rule," said Grami. "Only an estimated 20 percent of the negative effect on the brain and body is due to the event itself; 80 percent is due to your perception of the event and the weight you place on it."

"I see," said Ethan. "I've never heard of that 20:80 Rule before."

"Even when you can't do anything about the 20 percent, you can do almost everything about the 80 percent, because your brain creates your own perceptions," said Grami.

"So, Aimi," said Ethan, thoughtfully. "I want to get this straight. When you did your deep breathing and changed what you were saying to yourself, you were managing the 80 percent. Is that correct?" Aimi nodded. "Brilliant!" said Ethan. "I may have learned more today than you *Mystery Club* kids! In fact, I'm quite sure I have."

The food was delicious. Ethan kept them entertained with stories about the Krystal Kaverns and how they had been discovered. "I have a little surprise for you," said Ethan, as they finished eating their meal. "Dessert is on me, and it's a good one."

And was it ever! A big apple cobbler, warm from the oven and mouthwateringly scrumptious.

"What are you going to do now, Ethan?" asked Stella, when the last bit of apple cobbler had disappeared from the baking dish. "Guide tourists on another tour?"

"Yours was the last tour for today," replied Ethan. "I'm going to think about that 20:80 Rule and practice giving positive one-step instructions to myself and to others. I want the tourists I take on tours to understand what I say quickly and easily." He smiled. "What are you all going to do next?"

"Get into the car and head straight for home," said Grami, smiling. "It's been quite an adventure, and we have a long drive ahead of us."

"As soon as we get there, I'll give Buddy-the-Beagle a good dinner," said Stella. "He'll be so happy to see us. He'll sing his *I'm-so-glad-you're home* howl."

"I'll feed my rabbits," said Tad.

"I plan to read more about bats," said Connor. "And help Tad count his kits, of course." Tad rolled his eyes.

"I'll write to my school friend and tell her all about today's adventures at the Krystal Kaverns," said Toni.

"I'm going to bed when we get home," said Aimi. "I'm glad I wasn't hurt when I slipped, but I'm very tired."

And that's exactly what they did.

A teen decided he wanted to take,
A joey back home—a piece of cake.
The problem was that little gem,
From start to stop created mayhem.

11—Invisible Antidote

"Guess what, Grami!" said Connor, excitedly. "Mom and Dad say I can have a pet!"

"How fun," said Grami. "What type of pet do you want?"

"Probably a lizard or an iguana," said Connor. "Or a joey from Australia. But I wouldn't have tried to stuff a little kangaroo in my carry-on and sneak it onto the plane to Canada like a teenager did yesterday."

"I'll bet that was an unwise choice," said Grami.

"The news anchor said that part way through the flight the teen decided to give his new pet a little stretch," continued Connor. "Turned out his new pet didn't want to sit still and be petted. One leap and that little joey was up on the back of a seat. Like a Mexican jumping bean, it was. Then it was mayhem. Complete and utter mayhem!"

"What does may-hem mean?" asked Stella. "It is sewing? I want to *know*." Everyone looked at Grami.

"It means chaos, havoc, disorder, bedlam, pandemonium, unmitigated disaster, and you-name-it," said Grami. "Continue with the story, Connor."

"The joey jumped over seats and passengers and vaulted off the shoulders of airline attendants. Finally it landed on the food cart and snatched several packets of peanuts and crackers, scattering the rest of the snacks to kingdom come." Picturing the mayhem in his mind's eye, Connor burst out laughing.

"Imagine the mess!" said Toni. "It's not funny and yet it's very funny!" She started laughing, too.

"That little joey hopped from the food to the beverage cart, sending bottles and cups flying  everywhere," Connor continued. "It leapfrogged all over the plane from first class through business, into economy, and back again. Some passengers screamed, a baby cried, and one lady fainted dead away, she did."

"I hope that joey didn't create mayhem all the way from Australia to Canada!" said Grami. "That is one long plane ride."

"Oh, it didn't," said Connor, cheerfully. "The purser spoke with the captain, who left the cockpit to assess the situation personally. He even laughed when the joey took a flying leap and knocked his cap off. The captain's cap, that is. The captain suggested that the purser put some peanuts on the lid of one of the toilets. When the joey hopped in to grab the peanuts, the purser slammed the door and locked it. That stow-away—no fault of its own—spent the rest of the trip in the loo."

"What is the loo?" asked Stella. "And what is a purr-sir? I want to *know*."

"The word *loo* is used in some countries when referring to the toilet or restroom, as some call it. The name *purser* goes way back to about the year 1040 and the Royal Navy," said Grami. "On merchant ships, the 'clerk of burser' as these individuals were originally called (now it's just 'purser'), was in charge of supplies—food, drink, clothing, bedding, and candles. And I suppose anything else that might be needed. On today's modern passenger ships," Grami continued, "the purser oversees general administration: fees and charges, currency exchange, and any other money-related needs of the passengers and crew."

"Oh, I get it," said Stella. "Purse *and* purser. You carry money in your purse."

"You may, but not me," said Tad, laughing.

"In this age of modern airplanes," said Grami, "the chief flight attendant is often called the purser. Duties include overseeing the other flight attendants and making sure that the passengers are comfortable and safe. The flight purser is also responsible for verifying that all safety procedures are followed and must complete detailed reports on any out-of-the-ordinary events."

"Oh my," said Aimi, laughing. "I can just imagine the reports that poor purser had to make about the joey incident and all the mayhem."

"I say, Connor. You might want to get a little dog," said Toni. "Like Buddy-the-Beagle or Diva-the-singer. Either of those would be a lot safer."

"I would have been frightened," said Aimi. "What if the joey had hurt a passenger? The teenager's parents might be in big trouble."

"If I were that boy's mother," said Stella, dramatically, "I would never *ever* forgive him for that stunt! Not ever in a million years!"

"Not so fast, my friend," said Grami, smiling.

"Everyone on planet earth makes mistakes. It's part of being human. I imagine the boy thought he had come up with a good idea. Remember, most people do the best they can at the time with what they know."

"Well, *I* would *never* have forgiven him!" Stella repeated, indignantly. "*Mayhem* indeed! He's lucky none of the passengers had a heart attack and died."

"You might want to rethink that perspective," said Grami. "Have you ever made a mistake?"

"Yeah, Stella," said Aimi, "what's the biggest mistake you ever made?" Stella did not answer. "I remember if you don't," said Aimi.

Stella opened her mouth and then shut it again. She squirmed in her bean bag chair. Finally, she said, "Well, once our mom said the car needed fuel, so I got the hose and filled the fuel tank with water. I, umm-m, thought the car ran on water." Stella hung her head.

"There you have it," said Grami. "Did your mom forgive you?" Stella nodded. "So do you think you could forgive your teenager for a stunt like sneaking a joey onto the plane?" Stella nodded, slowly.

"I'm glad," said Grami. "Studies on forgiveness find that people tend to be healthier *and* happier when they forgive their own mistakes, as well as those of others."

A great deal of conversation and hilarity followed as the five *LM Club* members and their sponsor talked about the joey incident, mistakes each of them had made—and forgiveness.

"Well," said Grami, finally, "we sure got today's laughs out of that little joey incident. Now, remind me. What is on the agenda for you this morning?"

"Oh!" cried Aimi, clapping her hands. "We are going to discuss what we want to do for the opening celebration of the *LM Club* treehouse."

"Let's get on with it," said Tad. "What with laughing so much about Connor's joey story, I have lots of energy to spend on planning."

"That's true," said Grami. "Mirthful laughter can increase a person's energy."

"And it helps me think I could forgive that teenager if he belonged to me," said Stella. "It's hard to stay mad when you're laughing."

"Connor and I play the recorder," said Toni. "Aimi and Stella play ukuleles, and Tad plays the guitar. Good thing we've been practicing all summer."

"Thanks for reminding us what instruments we play," said Tad, laughing. "But, what's your point?"

"Do you remember the camping song Grami taught us, 'There's a Hole in the Bottom of the Sea'?" asked Toni.

"Yes," said Stella. "It was fun to sing."

"Aimi and I have been writing a song something like that," said Toni. "We call it the 'Treehouse Song.'"

"Toni and I will sing the first verse for you," said Aimi. The words go like this:

There's a house perched up in a tree in Grami's yard. Perched up in a tree is a house in Grami's yard. There's a house, there's a house. There's a house perched up in a tree in Grami's yard.

"That will be a great cumulative song for the open-house celebration," said Grami. "Good job!"

"I added a rug in the house perched up in a tree in Grami's yard," said Toni.

"And I added: 'a chair on the rug,'" said Aimi.

"How about 'a sleuth in the chair on the rug'?" asked Tad. Connor and Tad happily exchanged fist pumps.

"I want 'a bed by the sleuth in the chair,' for Buddy-the-Beagle," said Stella

"And then you'll have to put 'a *dog* in the bed . . .'" began Connor, and everyone burst out laughing. Connor and Tad laughed so hard they fell right down on the floor and laughed until the tears ran down their cheeks.

"I'm afraid I'll forget the words," said Aimi, when they had finally stopped laughing. "Singing and playing at the same time is complicated."

"You'll have time to practice playing your ukulele and singing," said Tad. "And we'll help you."

"But I'm still scared," said Aimi.

"Remember the stage in your brain?" asked Grami. "Fear has come out on stage and has sent joy to the wings."

"Oh, yes. Remind me what to do," said Aimi.

"Use the invisible antidote," said Grami.

"I saw an animal program where the doctor gave an *antidote* to a child with a snake bite," said Connor. "The antidote helped neutralize the poison."

"Exactly," said Grami. "Turns out there is an antidote for fear. It's gratitude…thankfulness…both types of joy. Fear cannot stay out on stage in your brain, Aimi, when you think of something for which to be grateful."

"I'm grateful," said Aimi. "I'm grateful that I'm a member of the *LM Club* and that we're going to have a treehouse."

"I'm grateful Grami let our dads and Uncle Bob build it in that huge tree in her big back yard," said Tad.

"I know a verse about gratitude," said Grami. "It goes like this: *There's an antidote for feeling bad, to use when you're afraid or sad. Just find one thing to be grateful for, and walk right thru that open door.*"

"Got it," Aimi said. "Okay: Aimi, *you* are singing the song *and* playing the ukulele at the same time."

Just then Grami's shiny blue cell phone rang.

"Hello," said Grami. "Yes, I am the *Longevity Mystery Club* sponsor, and yes, I did make that request." *Pause.* "Captain Bill? Did you say Captain *Bill*? What in

169

heaven's name are you doing at *our* Fire Station?" Grami exclaimed.

At that, all five *LM Club* members stopped talking and listened intently. "Yes," Grami continued. "That would be wonderful." *Pause.* "Oh, you could do it today? Right after lunch, you say? Absolutely, we can be there." *Pause.* "Thank you very much, Captain Bill. We'll see you at two o'clock. Today. Yes, I'm looking forward to it, as well."

Grami clicked off her shiny blue cell phone and looked at her watch. "Quick! To the kitchen on the double. We have work to do." The five sleuths looked at Grami, wide eyed, and then followed her into the kitchen. "An old high school friend of mine is consulting at our Fire Station for a month. He loves Florentines. They can bake while we eat lunch." Grami was already getting out bowls and cookie sheets.

"Florentines?" asked Tad. "You only make them for very special occasions. Is this a *very* special occasion?" Grami nodded and smiled.

Two hours later Grami and five sleuths went out to the car. Tad and Connor carefully placed a box of Florentines in the trunk. "Hop in and let's go," said Grami. Before long she turned the car into a side street.

"Oh, look," said Stella. "There's a bright yellow fire engine. It's almost sigh-ka-del-ik. And I know what that word means." Everyone laughed.

"And there are two red fire trucks," said Tad.

"Some fire stations are switching the color of their fire engines to bright yellow to help others see them more easily," said Grami. "Studies have shown that yellow is the first color distinguished in the left hemisphere of the brain." She parked the car, and everyone got out.

Just then a tall man in a uniform stepped out of the Fire Station and waved to Grami. "Hello, Captain Bill," said Grami. "Allow me to introduce you to the five members of the *Longevity Mystery Club*—of which I am sponsor: Aimi and Stella, Tad and Toni, and Connor."

"And, Sir, here is something Grami made for you," said Tad. Connor and Tad handed the box to Captain Bill.

"We all helped," said Toni.

Captain Bill opened the box and stared down at two dozen Florentines. "As I live and breathe," he whispered.

"They're really good, Sir," said Connor.

"I know, I know," said Captain Bill. "But I haven't had Florentines for years and years. Your Grami and I went to the same school when we were kids. She liked to cook and sometimes she brought Florentines for a special treat. If these are anything like what she used to bake, they will be wonderful!"

"I bet she's an even better cook now," said Aimi. "We're learning to be healthier so we can live longer."

"Well, now," said Captain Bill, as he led the way into the Fire Station. "I'm very glad to hear that. Come, along. I see I have my work cut out for me today." In a large room with fire-fighting equipment hanging on the walls, Captain Bill placed the box on a table. "You will forgive me for helping myself to one of these before we get started," he said, looking at Grami. "It's been a very long time since I tasted your Florentines."

"Have several," said Stella. "There are *two* dozen."

"I may do just that," said Captain Bill, taking a big bite. "Out of this world!" And he took another big bite.

"It was a huge surprise to learn that you were consulting at our Fire Station," said Grami. "That gave me the idea to make Florentines for old time's sake."

Captain Bill crunched into another Florentine and waved everyone to chairs. "Every bit as good as I remember, if not better," he said, between bites. "Now, if I understand correctly, there'll soon be a treehouse perched up in a tree in Grami's big back yard. My job today is to teach you how to climb a ladder safely."

"I already know how to climb a ladder," said Stella.

"Do you, now," said Captain Bill. "Tell me."

Stella stood first on one foot, then on the other. Finally she said, "I guess I don't know how to tell you. I just know how to do it."

"Part of really knowing how to do something safely is being able to tell another person how to do it," said Captain Bill, smiling. "By the time we're done, young lady, you'll not only know how to do it yourself but also how to teach others." He took a third Florentine and then put the box on the top shelf of a tall cupboard, adding, "I'm not ready to share these yet—if ever. Now, follow me." Captain Bill opened a door into a yard enclosed with chain-link fencing. "Many people fall from ladders because they don't know ladder safety. This is our ladder and fire-safety classroom." There were several tall ladders,

a square tower, a shed, and a bright red fire truck. Captain Bill pointed to a ladder leaning against the chain-link fence. "This ladder here is 12 feet (3.5 meters) tall. The bottom needs to angle out from the fence one third of its height."

"That's four feet," said Toni. "A smidgen or two over a meter."

"Correct," said Captain Bill, chuckling. "Make sure the ladder is firmly positioned on solid ground and that there are no electrical wires overhead or close by. It's a good idea to have another person hold onto the ladder, too. Would you like to go first, Stella?"

"Yes, Sir," said Stella. "I'd like my big sister, Aimi, to hold the ladder." Captain Bill nodded, so Aimi stepped forward and held one side of the ladder with both hands.

"Now, Stella," said Captain Bill, "face the ladder and stand in the middle. Always use a three-point contact system when climbing: two hands and a foot *or* two feet and a hand on the ladder. Only stand on the top step if the ladder is clearly marked saying that is safe. Ready?" Stella nodded. "Put your foot on the first step and both hands on the ladder." Stella did so. "Pull yourself up so both feet are on the first step." Stella did that, too. "Check," said Captain Bill. "Now, move your hands up and put one foot on the next rung of the ladder."

"So far, so good," said Captain Bill. "Check after each step to be sure you are safe."

"Stella climbed nearly to the top of the ladder.

"Good work," said Captain Bill. "Now reverse the process and come down. *Slowly*."

Stella climbed down, repeating: "Two hands and a foot *or* two feet and a hand on the ladder at all times."

"You learn quickly," said Captain Bill. "Each one of you pick a ladder and go through the same process."

"This is fun," said Tad. "I never knew there were rules for climbing a ladder. What else do we need to know, Captain Bill?"

"Never *ever* build a fire in the treehouse," Captain Bill said. "And be extremely careful when you transfer *from* the ladder *to* the treehouse."

Each person climbed a ladder, being careful to follow the rules. Even Grami. "Good thing you wore slacks today," said Connor. Grami smiled.

"Ordinarily, this bright red practice fire engine isn't open to the general public," said Captain Bill. "Today it is—in exchange for a couple dozen Florentines." Five *LM Club* members clapped their hands. One even jumped up in the air and twirled three times.

Captain Bill led the five sleuths and Grami to the bright red fire engine. "This is now our 'training dummy,'" he said. "The yellow engine is our new one. Up the ladder you go," he said, encouragingly. "Follow the rules."

Grami and the five sleuths spent nearly an hour investigating every nook and cranny of the bright red fire engine. They took turns sitting in the driver's seat and then standing in the crow's nest at the back. They learned where the whistle was located and how it operated. They saw the special equipment lockers and what they contained.

"This was great fun, Sir," said Connor. "I've been thinking about being a veterinarian—but riding a truck to fight fires might be pretty exciting."

"We always need qualified vets who can help us care for injured animals," said Captain Bill. "That's pretty exciting, too." Connor nodded.

"I hope Connor becomes a vet," said Tad, "so he can give my rabbits any medical care they need."

"Our *LM Club* treehouse is almost done," said Stella. "Connor's dad, the twins' dad, and Uncle Bob are building it for us. Would you come to our open house?"

"And would you wear your uniform?" asked Connor. "It's really cool."

"We'd make you more Florentines," said Toni, looking over at Grami.

"Bribing me with Florentines, are you?" asked Captain Bill, laughing. Toni and Stella nodded, seriously. "Well, I'd be delighted to attend—in my uniform. And I know your Uncle Bob. It'll be good to see him again."

"Thank you," cried the five sleuths in unison. Once in Grami's car, they waved good-bye to Captain Bill.

"We need to finish planning the celebration for our treehouse," said Aimi, as they drove toward home.

"I *know*," said Toni. "We've got to get with it!"

And that's exactly what they did.

The LM Club treehouse is finally done!
We think it's the best one under the sun.
Our celebration was second to none—
And everyone had a barrel of fun.

12—Stellar Celebration

 "Grami," said Tad, coming into the kitchen, "whoever snuck the letter *S* into 'fast food' was pretty sneaky. It's really *fat* food. Some kids at my school eat a lot of fast food, and they're already overweight." Tad looked approvingly at the platters of food on the kitchen counter. Orange and purple carrot sticks, hummus and guacamole, baked chips made from whole ancient grains and seeds, celery sticks—some with peanut butter. "Oh, goody," he said. "Watermelon radishes!"

"Watermelon radishes?" asked Stella. "What are watermelon radishes? I want to *know*."

"They're a special type of radish," said Grami. "Some think they look a bit like miniature watermelons."

"They certainly do not taste like watermelon," said Stella, biting into a colorful radish. "Watermelon is juicy. These are crunchy!"

"I'm so-o-o glad we're serving healthy food at the *LM Club* treehouse celebration," said Aimi.

"And for special dessert, there are dozens of Florentines hidden in the pantry," said Toni.

"And pitchers of water with lemon-juice ice cubes and floating lemon slices," said Aimi.

"I like the menu you've selected," said Grami, "and how you have all pitched in to get things ready."

"Here's the white ribbon," said Connor, "and scissors, of course. Our sponsor is going to do the honors." Grami smiled.

"Who'll hold the ribbon?" asked Stella.

"Well, now," said Grami, "I don't think we've figured that out yet."

"Let's put all our names in a hat and draw two," said Aimi. "The two whose names are drawn will hold the white ribbon."

"You can use my hat," said Tad. "It'll hold five names nicely. I have a small head." Everyone laughed.

"Your head is no smaller than any of ours," said Connor, laughing. "You are so funny, Tad."

"Can we put Buddy-the-Beagle's name in the hat?" asked Stella. "After all, he is the *LM Club* mascot."

Tad shook his head. "Really Stella, how in the wide-wide world do you think Buddy-the-Beagle could hold one end of the ribbon? I mean, use your brain, girl!"

"I was just joking," said Stella, laughing. "I know Buddy-the-Beagle will just tear around Grami's back yard with one end of the white ribbon in his mouth, if he gets a hold on it, that is. But if his name *had* gone into the hat and he *had* been selected, I'd have had to hold the ribbon *for* him!"

"Ah-ha! So that was the 'method to your madness,' as the saying goes," said Connor, laughing.

"Pretty clever, Stella." said Toni, also laughing.

"But it's not going to work," said Aimi.

"In a way there are *seven* sleuths," said Connor, seriously. "Grami is our sponsor and a 'researching sleuth.' Buddy-the-Beagle is our mascot and a 'sniffing sleuth.'"

"True," said Grami, "but let's draw only from the five actual *Longevity Mystery Club* members." Everyone agreed, so Grami wrote the name of each *Club* member on a piece of paper, folded each in half, and put it in the cap that Tad held.

"Close your eyes, Grami," said Tad, "and pull two names out of the hat." Grami did just that.

"Let me read them," cried Stella. "I'm the littlest!" Grami handed her the two pieces of paper. "Connor," read Stella, as everyone

clapped. "And. . ." she unfolded the second paper, "Toni!" Everyone clapped again.

"Okay," said Grami, "as your sponsor, let's briefly go over the program as you've planned it. First, the *LM*

Club members welcome the guests and show them into the back yard. At two o'clock, the club sponsor..."

"That's you, Grami," Stella interrupted.

"She knows that," said Aimi. "Please, Stella, just listen for once." Stella nodded and listened.

"The *Club* sponsor," continued Grami, keeping her face straight, "tells the assembled guests how the idea for a treehouse got started and thanks the two dads and Uncle Bob for building such a fine structure. Then she thanks Captain Bill for teaching the *LM Club* members the proper way to climb a ladder and giving them tips on treehouse safety."

Stella was so excited she clapped her hands, jumped up in the air, and twirled three times, but she didn't say anything. Buddy-the-Beagle also jumped up in the air, and fortunately he didn't say anything either.

"So far, so good?" asked Grami, looking around.

The five *LM Club* members nodded. "Next, you'll get your instruments and perform the '122 Song.' Then it will be time for Connor and Toni to carry out the white ribbon with a huge bow tied in the middle. They'll each hold one end so that the ribbon is in front of the ladder that goes up to the treehouse."

"We'll have to stand there a while," said Connor. "I'm sure everyone will want to take pictures."

"And after the ribbon is cut," said Aimi, "Toni will announce the 'Treehouse Song.'"

"And we'll all sing while Tad plays the guitar," said Connor.

"That song is a hoot," said Toni. "I really hope I can get through it without laughing."

"Toni," said Aimi, seriously, "you know how to do that. You tell yourself: 'Toni, you are singing the song all the way through and laughing afterward.' You can do this."

"You're getting good at this new way of talking, Aimi," said Tad. Aimi smiled.

"And when that's done," said Grami, "the two neighbor ladies—who offered to help, thank heavens—will bring out platters of food and jugs of lemon water and put them on the two picnic tables that have been set out."

"Then everyone will eat," said Tad. "Funny that *I* should think of that," at which Connor laughed so hard he nearly fell over.

"And after everyone has eaten, we'll take turns touring guests through the treehouse," said Stella. "This celebration is going to be so much fun! I can hardly wait."

Grami looked at the clock. "I think that does it," she said. "I'm proud of you, and it *will be* a fun celebration."

"Let's go sing our songs through one more time," said Aimi.

"While I go and change into my new pants suit," said Grami. "Two sizes smaller than what I was wearing at the beginning of the summer, mind you."

The five sleuths clapped and smiled. Buddy-the-Beagle did not clap or smile. He snored.

"Grami, Grami," called Stella about ten minutes later. "A red fire truck just pulled up in front of the house and *three* people are getting out. Come quick!"

The five members of *Longevity Mystery Club* and their sponsor, plus their mascot, all trooped out to the front yard to see what was happening.

"Hello, all you sleuths," called Captain Bill, shutting the door of the red fire truck. "As promised, I'm here for the celebration and dressed in my uniform. Plus, I brought Mayor Lind and Howard, a reporter from the newspaper. I figured we might as well do this up right and get ourselves in the news."

Captain Bill introduced Grami, the five sleuths, and their mascot to Mayor Lind and then to Howard, the newspaper reporter who was a very tall young man indeed.

"I'm always looking for good stories about doings in our very own town," said Howard, smiling down at the five *LM Club* members from his very tall height. "And I see that your mascot even has a uniform. Well, sort of."

Howard the newspaper reported laughed and laughed. At that, Buddy-the-Beagle sat down on the ground, put his little head back, pointed his little nose into the air, and howled.

"That's his *I'm-happy-to-be-here* howl," explained Stella.

"Oh," said Captain Bill, "I thought maybe that was Buddy-the-Beagle's *I'm-happy-you-are-here* howl."

"He's our club mascot," said Stella, importantly, "so naturally he is wearing his mascot tog. Do you see the letters *LMC* printed on it? That's short for the *Longevity Mystery Club*, and I'm the littlest member. Buddy-the-beagle is not a regular member, but he can sleuth with his nose."

"Really, Stella," said Connor, quite seriously. "Whatever would he sleuth with except his nose? He's a beagle, for heaven's sake. Think, girl."

Evidently, Howard, the very tall newspaper reporter thought that comment was extremely funny, too, because he kept slapping his long leg and laughing.

A few minutes later the two dads and Uncle Bob arrived, accompanied by their wives.

"As I live and breathe," said Uncle Bob, walking up to Captain Bill and holding out his hand, "if it isn't Billy in person!"

"*Captain Bill* to you, *Bobby*," said Captain Bill, laughing, and shaking Uncle Bob's hand. "And I don't even want to know how many years it's been since we've seen each other."

"Let's just agree to let the exact number slide," Uncle Bob replied. "You may remember that math was never my best subject. Let's just say it's been a few and leave it at that." Both men laughed and high fived each other, while the others laughed.

Uncle Bill introduced Mayor Lind and Howard to Uncle Bob, after which Uncle Bob introduced the three wives and the two dads, explaining that they had helped build the treehouse. (The dads, not the wives.) Almost immediately they started talking about the treehouse and what a great idea it was. Soon other neighbors and friends began  to arrive and, as planned, the *LM Club* members took turns guiding them to Grami's big back yard.

"Aimi," said Grami, as the guests were helping themselves to lemon water from the pitchers that the neighbor ladies had already set out on the picnic tables, "please go to my sewing room and bring back two more pairs of scissors. I'm going to invite Captain Bill and Mayor Lind to cut the ribbon with me."

"What a good idea," cried Aimi. "I'm sure they'll do it. I think the Mayor always likes to have her picture in the newspaper and on television."

From an open window Grami heard the sound of the antique grandfather clock striking two. (Earlier the clockmaker's assistant had come to the house and fixed the clock so she was pretty confident that it really was two o'clock.) Grami clapped her hands and the buzz of conversation quieted. Then she told the assembled guests about the *Longevity Mystery Club*, the idea for a club treehouse, and thanked Uncle Bob and the two dads for building it.

"Thank *you* for buying the new building materials," said Aimi, in her soft voice.

Grami smiled and nodded. "And now," she announced, "here are the five members of the *Longevity Mystery Club* to debut their new club song."

Aimi sang and played on her ukulele. So did Stella. Tad strummed on his guitar and sang, too. Connor and

Toni did not sing because they were playing their recorders. When they finished performing the '122 Song' the guests clapped and clapped, and the five sleuths took a bow.

Next, Toni and Connor each took one end of the white ribbon and held it so the large white bow was in front of the ladder to the new *LM Club* treehouse. Buddy-the-Beagle took one look at the large white bow and promptly trotted over and sat down underneath it.

"It is my great pleasure to have Mayor Lind and Captain Bill cut the ribbon with me," said Grami.

Aimi carefully handed scissors to all three.

"Hold it, hold it," called Howard, the very tall reporter. "I'd like to have the other three club members in the picture, too."

So Tad stood next to Toni, Aimi stood beside Connor, and Stella ran over to be near Aimi. Buddy-the-Beagle sat under the big white bow right in front of Grami.

"Our Buddy-the-Beagle wants to be right in the middle of everything," Stella whispered to Aimi.

"Count us off, Uncle Bob," Captain Bill called. "Remember how you used to do that for the younger grades during track 'n field meets? Of course, that *was* a hundred years ago."

"Sure thing," said Uncle Bob, laughing. "Glad to. On your mark, get set . . ." he began.

"But there is no 'mark,'" cried Stella, interrupting. "This is not track 'n field. It's a Stellar Celebration!"

"Right you are," said Uncle Bob, trying hard to keep his face straight. "Let's try this: one for the money, two for the show, three to get ready, and four to go. CUT!"

Three pairs of scissors went snip, snip, snip as pieces of white ribbon floated to the ground. The big white ribbon bow fell right on top of Buddy-the-Beagle, completely hiding him from view. Howard, the newspaper reporter laughed so hard Grami thought he might drop his camera. There was a great deal of clapping and whistling. Then Grami announced that after the next song, refreshments would be available--and, after that, tours through the *Longevity Mystery Club* treehouse perched up in the tree in Grami's big yard.

The five sleuths sang the 'Treehouse Song' while Tad played the guitar.

"Capital song!" Captain Bill shouted. "Sing it again, and we'll sing with you." They did, and then they were asked to do it a *third* time. "I want to record that," said

Captain Bill, "so I can take a CD back to the school where my wife teaches. Fact is, I know a guy who owns a studio here in town, and I'll arrange for a recording session."

Of course the *LM Club* members were very excited. Aimi jumped up and down and up and down. Stella clapped her hands, jumped up in the air, and twirled three times. Tad and Connor high-fived each other, and Toni did a handstand. Buddy-the-Beagle crawled out from under the big white bow, pointed his little nose in the air, and howled his *I'm-a-happy-dog* howl.

"Aimi composed both our songs," Toni told the guests. Of course, everyone clapped again.

Aimi bowed and said, "Thank you. Grami told me I could do it, and Toni and my music teacher both helped."

"Your team effort was obviously successful," said Mayor Lind, shaking hands with the five *LM Club* members. She did not shake hands with Buddy-the-Beagle, their mascot. After climbing out from under the big white bow, he had wandered off in search of his water dish.

"Time for refreshments," announced Grami, "and many thanks to our two wonderful neighbors for their help!"

"Purple carrot sticks and watermelon radishes?" asked Howard, the very tall newspaper reporter. "I need pictures of those. Talk about colorful!"

And Howard snapped happily away at the picnic tables covered with attractive platters of delicious food.

The guests helped themselves to the refreshments and ate and talked and talked and ate and looked at the treehouse perched up in the tree in Grami's big yard. When a great deal of food had disappeared from the two picnic tables, a platter of Florentines arrived.

"I sure could get used to these again," said Captain Bill, patting his stomach. "In about one nanosecond!"

"Grami made them as an extra special treat because you used to have them when you were kids," said Stella, seriously. "Usually we only make them for holiday dinner because they aren't really very healthy, and we all want to live a very very *very* long time."

Captain Bill nodded, patted Stella's shoulder, and said, "I like the way you five sleuths and Grami are thinking. Put that into practice like you did when learning your songs, and you'll be well on your way to longevity."

"Time for treehouse tours," called Uncle Bob. "Anyone who wants to climb the ladder can do so now, five or six at a time."

"Pictures! I need pictures *first*!" shouted Howard, the very tall reporter.

"Let Stella climb partway up the ladder for the picture," suggested Captain Bill. "She was the first sleuth to climb the ladder at the Fire Station."

Stella walked to the foot of the ladder and looked up. "It looks like a long way," she said, with hesitation.

"Just climb up half-way to begin with," said Howard, "and the rest of you line up at the bottom."

Stella stood in the middle and put two hands on the ladder. "I'll hold the ladder for you," said Mayor Lind.

Stella put one foot on the first rung. Then using the three-point contact system that Captain Bill had taught

them, she started climbing. "Two hands and a foot *or* two feet and a hand on the ladder at all times," she repeated to herself.

Half-way up, with two feet and one hand on the ladder, Stella half turned and waved her other hand.

"Great pictures!" said Howard, excitedly. "Hold that pose, young lady. You look great. So do you, Mayor Lind. I'll snap a couple more shots. These will look great in the newspaper. Just great!"

"They'll look great on the six o'clock evening news, too," said a young man coming around the corner of the house into Grami's big back yard. "I'm Lee, from the TV station. Howard here just texted me about this Stellar Celebration. Hold your pose." Quickly setting up his equipment, Lee started taking pictures and more pictures,

but no one seemed to mind. Buddy-the-Beagle even made it into a couple of shots, dragging the big white bow with him. When someone told Lee about the two new songs, he made Stella climb down from the ladder, so he could record the five sleuths performing both songs again.

"Catchy tunes," Lee said, when the children had finished. "I was so busy listening I nearly forgot to film." He laughed and everyone clapped again.

Finally, with the songs all recorded and the pictures all snapped, the guests took turns touring through the treehouse. They loved it and were profuse with their compliments to the builders. Then there were trips back to the picnic tables for more refreshments.

Grami gave Buddy-the-Beagle a special dog treat to chew on. "To keep him out from under everyone's feet," she said. Sure enough, their mascot settled himself under a picnic table and chewed and chewed and chewed. It kept him very busy—as long as the special dog treat lasted.

Finally, it was time for the guests to leave. There was a great deal of hand-shaking and clapping each other on the back. Even Buddy-the-Beagle got a few pats on the head and some 'Good dog' comments.

Mayor Lind said, "This is one of the most fun functions I've been to this year. Thanks for inviting me, Captain Bill."

"We'd have invited you ourselves," said Stella, "if we'd known you wanted to come." That comment triggered a great deal of merriment.

Howard, the very tall newspaper reporter and Lee, the photographer from the TV station, packed up their gear and left. Uncle Bob and the two dads and all three wives waved good-bye and went home. Little by little the other guests said their good-byes until only the five *LM Club* members, their sponsor, and the club mascot were left. Plus the two neighbor ladies, of course, who had been such a great help.

"I simply don't know how we'd have managed without you," said Grami. "And look, you've already put away most of the stuff while we were saying good-byes."

192

"There wasn't much left to put away," said one of the neighbor ladies, laughing. "Your guests pretty well picked the platters clean."

"You're most welcome," said the other neighbor. "After all, what are good neighbors for? You'd have done the same for us. Plus, we had fun, too."

Long after the guests had left and everything had been cleaned up and put away, the five members of the *LM Club*, their sponsor, and their mascot hung out in the new *LM Club* treehouse. Grami had had no trouble climbing the ladder. She'd even carried Buddy-the-Beagle up with her in a little beagle backpack, a gift from Captain Bill. "It's the safest way to get your little roly-poly mascot up and down the ladder," Captain Bill had said. "He's far too little to climb up or get down on his own."

Grami and the five sleuths, comfortable on their bean bags, talked about everything that had happened at the open house, and then they talked about it again. Gradually the sun slipped below the horizon and the moon took its place. Buddy-the-Beagle, curled in his basket lair beside Grami's rocking chair, snored softly.

"I'll bet that dog is dreaming about the big white bow," said Connor. "He hauled that thing all around the yard for hours. Actually, it's a gray color now."

"It was a stellar celebration," said Stella. "Do you get it? *Stellar*. It's mostly my name *Stella*." She laughed.

"We got it," said Toni, smiling.

"How could we miss it?" asked Tad, chuckling.

"*Stellar*? Oh, for heaven's sake, Stella," Aimi said and then burst out laughing, too.

"You are incorrigible, Stella," said Connor, also chuckling. "Absolutely incorrigible."

"I even know what that means," said Stella, saucily. "Captain Bill called me an 'incorrigible optimist.' He said that I was always cheerful."

"I'm not sure that's exactly . . ." began Connor, but this time Grami interrupted.

"Close enough," Grami said, still laughing herself. "Close enough." Connor nodded that he understood.

"Grami, it's almost time for school to start again," said Aimi. "This has been the best--and I mean the *best*-- summer of my whole life. Thank you for being such a *stellar* sponsor. Do you get it, Stella?" Aimi asked, mischievously. "*Stellar* sponsor."

Everyone had another good laugh about that one, including Stella. Even Buddy-the-Beagle woke up, stuck his little nose in the air and howled his *I'm-happy-to-be-here* howl. Then he promptly put his head down and went right back to sleep. And back to snoring.

"It seems like a long time since we first talked about being detectives," said Grami. "But it's only been one summer. I feel like a different person now."

"Well, you've lived a Longevity Lifestyle for nearly an entire summer," said Aimi, laughing. "Just wait until it's been a whole year and then two whole years. You may even start getting younger!"

"I want to get *older*," said Stella, "and grow *taller*— so my head will reach the cross-bar and I can go on the new 'Red Roller' ride. But," and here Stella paused rather dramatically, "I *also* want to live a very very *very* long time and be a supercentenarian."

"Here, here," said Connor, as he and Tad high-fived.

"*And* we all selected a club name and a sponsor and a mascot and wrote a club song," said Toni, sleepily.

"We composed a cumulative song, too," said Aimi, "although the 'Treehouse Song' was actually easier to write." Aimi and Toni smiled at each other.

"Remember when Grami got a new computer?" said Conner. "Then, we could sleuth at home and not have to  go to the Neo-Leo Wordpark—unless of course we all wanted to research on our own computer at the same time."

"I still love that new name," said Aimi. "The Neo-Leo Wordpark. That 21st century 'Librivox' library is also one of my favorite adventures. There is so much to see and do there."

"Grami, can the *LM Club* keep on meeting after school starts?" asked Stella, stretching and yawning. "After all, we have a *Club* treehouse now."

"What does having a treehouse have to do with it?" asked Aimi. Stella shrugged and yawned again.

"I'd like that," said Tad, also stretching and yawning. "I've learned a lot this summer, and we had so much fun. You planned *stellar* adventures, Grami."

"Oh, let's do," said Toni. "Can we Grami? I'd like that. We're all healthier, you know, and smarter, too." And then Toni yawned.

"Definitely!" agreed Connor. "I want to keep on being a detective, sleuthing and learning and learning and sleuthing." Just then Connor yawned. Twice, in fact.

"I think we could probably fit in a meeting of the LMC once a week," said Grami, "although we might have to schedule an adventure once a month instead of every week . . ." And wouldn't you know it, Grami yawned and then so did Toni.

"Just until next summer," said Stella, herself yawning. "An adventure once a month just until next summer. After that we can have an adventure every week!"

"This yawning business is catching," said Aimi. "Even Buddy-the-Beagle is yawning. And yawning, and yawning!"

Grami watched Buddy-the-Beagle yawn and yawn and yawn. When Grami herself yawned, she said, "Okay, *LM Club* members. All this yawning is telling my brain that it's time for our Stellar Celebration to wind itself up for today. Your sponsor's opinion is that we need to put Buddy-the-Beagle in his backpack, climb down from this new *LM*

Club treehouse, and go to bed. We can make more plans tomorrow."

"I'll bet that tonight we all dream about today," said Connor, smiling, as they made their way to the house.

And that's exactly what they did.

Our club meets in the treehouse now.
When visitors see it they say, "Oh, Wow!"
We're lucky to have this stellar suite—
Plus sponsor and mascot can't be beat.

LM Club Song

La da da da da da da!
I am on a longevity journey,
Learning how to become a healthier me.
From here on out I'll find the key
To be the best that I can be.
I am on a longevity journey!
La da da da da da da!

> *Longevity Club is fun and new,*
> *Longevity sleuthing is good for you,*
> *Longevity living is what I choose to do—*
> *To help me be happy and healthy, too.*

La da da da da da da!
I can live a Longevity Lifestyle,
I've been doing it now for quite a while.
I always tell myself each day,
I'm a winner in every way.
I can live a Longevity Lifestyle!
La da da da da da da!

Longevity Club is fun and new,
Longevity sleuthing is good for you,
Longevity living is what I choose to do—
To help me be happy and healthy, too.

La da da da da da da!
I really really really really love my longevity journey,
For the rest of my life that's what I will be,
A whole lot better in every way,
And getting healthier every day.
I really really really really love my longevity journey!
La da da da da da da!

Longevity Club is fun and new,
Longevity sleuthing is good for you,
Longevity living is what I choose to do—
To help me be happy and healthy, too.

LMC Treehouse Song

There's a house perched up in a tree in Grami's yard
Perched up in a tree is a house in Grami's yard
There's a house, there's a house,
There's a house perched up in a tree in Grami's yard

There's a rug in the house perched up in the tree in
Grami's yard
On the floor there's a rug in the house perched up in the
tree in Grami's yard
There's a rug, there's a rug,
There's a rug in the house perched up in the tree in
Grami's yard

There's a chair on the rug in the house perched up in the
tree in Grami's yard
Right there is a chair on the rug in the house perched up
in the tree in Grami's yard
There's a chair, there's a chair,
There's a chair on the rug in the house perched up in the
tree in Grami's yard

There's a sleuth on the chair on the rug in the house
perched up in the tree in Grami's yard
Curled up is a sleuth on the chair on the rug in the house
perched up in the tree in Grami's yard

There's a sleuth, there's a sleuth,
There's a sleuth on the chair on the rug in the house
perched up in the tree in Grami's yard

There's a bed by the sleuth on the chair on the rug in the house perched up in the tree in Grami's yard
Right close is a bed by the sleuth on the chair on the rug in the house perched up in the tree in Grami's yard
There's a bed, there's a bed,
There's a bed by the sleuth on the chair on the rug in the house perched up in the tree in Grami's yard

There's a dog in the bed by the sleuth on the chair on the rug in the house perched up in the tree in Grami's yard
Asleep in the bed is a dog by the sleuth on the chair on the rug in the house perched up in the tree in Grami's yard
There's a dog, there's a dog,
There's a dog in the bed by the sleuth on the chair on the rug in the house perched up in the tree in Grami's yard

There's a dog,
There's a bed
There's a sleuth,
There's a chair
There's a rug,
There's a house
Perched up in the tree
In Grami's yard!

The Longevity Club is fun, 'tis true,
Longevity sleuthing is good for you,
Longevity living we choose to do—
To help us be happy and healthy, too.

At birth you get just one of each,
A brain and body to train and teach.
Take good care and you'll be glad—
Brain replacements aren't to be had!

Sharlet M. Briggs, PhD

Sharlet M. Briggs has an infectious *'this can be done and it's not as hard as you-think'* attitude, along with an ability to empower individuals to change their perception and as a result change their realities. This has made her a sought-after speaker, mentor and author.

Briggs has a passion for healthcare and speaks internationally, sharing brain-function and healthcare information in a practical, engaging, and enlightening style. She is Market President and Chief Executive Officer for Kern County, California, including Adventist Health Bakersfield and Adventist Health Tehachapi Valley.

In addition, she enjoys educating adults, youth, and children about the brain and brain function. She has authored and co-authored books and DVD's. She is especially interested in writing stories that can help children learn about the brain and Emotional Intelligence Quotient or EQ early in life.

Briggs has an earned doctorate in Clinical Psychology.

Contact Dr. Briggs at www.thrivingbrain.com

Arlene R. Taylor, PhD

Arlene R. Taylor, sometimes referred to as the *brain guru*, is an internationally known author and presenter. A sought-after speaker, she has spoken to thousands, providing practical brain function information in educational, entertaining, and empowering ways.

Taylor is founder and president of Realizations Inc, a non-profit corporation that engages in brain function research and provides related educational resources. A member of the *National Speakers Association* and listed with the *Professional Speakers Bureau International*, she has a Master's with a double major and two earned doctorates.

Access Taylor's weekday brain blog from her website homepage (www.arlenetaylor.org) or from the Longevity Lifestyle Matters website (www.LLM.life) or have it sent directly to your phone or email. You may also sign up to receive SynapSez®, her free quarterly online Brain Bulletin.

Contact Dr. Taylor at: www.ArleneTaylor.org

Books and Audiobooks

- *Age-Proofing Your Brain—21 Factors You Can Control,* 2nd Edition (paperback, eBook, audiobook) Taylor & Briggs

- *Age-Proofing Your Memory—Ultimate,* 2nd Edition (paperback, eBook) Taylor & Briggs

  Three additional editions are available:

  - *Age-Proofing Your Memory... Scripture* Edition. Exercises differ from Ultimate edition. Some of the brain aerobic exercises draw on names and terminology used in scripture. References to denominational dogma and specific theological perspectives are avoided.

  - *Age-Proofing Your Memory...Mormon* Edition. Exercises differ from Ultimate edition. Some of the brain aerobic exercises are based on King James Version names and terminology and on *The Book of Mormon.*

  - *Age-Proofing Your Memory...Catholic* Edition. Exercises differ different from Ultimate edition. Some of the brain aerobic exercises are based on scriptural references from *The Holy Bible, Revised Standard Version, Second Catholic Edition* (with ecclesiastical approval of the United States Conference of Catholic Bishops), 1966 Edition; revised according to the *LITURIAM AUTHENTICAM,* 2002.

- *Adventures of Aimi* (paperback, eBook, audiobook) Taylor & Briggs

- *Adventures of Stella* (paperback, eBook, audiobook) Taylor & Briggs

- *Adventures of the Longevity Mystery Club* (paperback, eBook, audiobook) Taylor & Briggs

- *Longevity Lifestyle Matters—How to stay healthier and younger for longer* (paperback, eBook, audiobook) Taylor with Horton & Briggs

- *Longevity Lifestyle Matters—Companion Notebook* (paperback, eBook, audiobook) Taylor with Horton & Briggs

- *Longevity Lifestyle Matters—Just the Facts!* (Paperback, eBook, Audiobook)Taylor with Horton

- *Beyond the House of Silence* (paperback, eBook) Taylor & Banford

- *Brain Benders - brain aerobic exercises* (paperback) Taylor

- *Chronicles of the Alabaster Owl* (paperback, eBook, audiobook) Taylor

- *Chronicles of the Littlest Dolphin* (paperback, eBook, audiobook) Taylor

- *Chronicles of the Jungle King* (paperback, eBook, audiobook) Taylor

- *I Chose Hope—and That Made the Difference* (paperback, eBook, audiobook) Taylor

- *Your Brain Has a Bent (Not a Dent) 3rd Edition* (paperback, eBook, audiobook) Taylor & Brewer

Paperbacks, audiobooks (CD and MP3 formats) and eBooks are available from and distributed through Pacific Health Education Center

www.pacifichealth.org or info@pacifichealth.org

Paperbacks, eBooks, and some DVDs are also available at Amazon.com and on Kindle

Authors & Resources